VAMPIRES, VCRS, AND VIOLENCE

BEWITCHER'S BEACH PARANORMAL COZY MYSTERIES
BOOK 5

EMILY FLUKE

ALSO BY EMILY FLUKE

Be sure to snag the prequels to both the Mari Fable Mysteries, and the Bewitcher's Beach Paranormal Cozy Mysteries FREE from my newsletter: The Glass Coffin and Be Careful What You Witch For.

https://landing.mailerlite.com/webforms/landing/y4h6c8

CAST OF CHARACTERS

Noema Wolf (temporary last name) Once werewolves are turned, they have no memory of their previous lives.

As a werewolf who can smell emotions and a lover of mystery movies, Noema finds herself sniffing out suspects whenever a troublesome visitor upsets her cozy, seaside town. But another case is not what this single mother of four, manager of Mockbuster Video Rental, and playwright needs thrown into her busy schedule.

Halen, Dio, Jovi, and Stevie Wolf:

These four mischievous 'pups' each help their mom solve mysteries or run the video rental shop in their own unique ways. As born werewolves, they don't experience memory loss —but as eight-year-olds, they suffer selective hearing when it comes to following the rules.

Sheriff Sett Lawrence:

This overprotective gargoyle takes life too seriously. His six-foot, six-inch stony body with muscular wings and horns does nothing to match his introverted, patient, and studious personality. But it certainly frightens visitors.

Crow:

A mysterious man with a handsome smirk. Crow took advantage of the low housing market in Bewitcher's Beach after a newcomer was recently murdered. This "tall dark" has plenty of secrets but isn't afraid to tease, flirt, and joke in the face of danger. And as hidden as he may seem—as the new owner of Roller Shakes—Crow socializes with the whole town on a regular basis.

Hattie Sharpe:

This harsh, flapper-girl starlet became a ghost in the height of the Roaring Twenties when her bold attitude landed her the target of a deadly Hollywood stunt. Now, she directs Everland Theater's plays and tells it like it is, no matter how many enemies it creates.

Chanel:

A gorgeous siren who runs the clothing boutique in Bewitcher's Beach. Her ability to give voice to songs that can temporarily control people only works on those who aren't in love.

Madam Rowena:

The chief academic officer at Shadowvale, Madam Rowena, is both harsh and brilliant. She is Noema's main point of contact with all the witches at Shadowvale studying *The Book of Prophecies* and working to recreate the protection spell.

CHAPTER 1
A RUDE AWAKENING

I WOKE up from a crashing sound with a scream on my lips. I wasn't normally the screaming type. As a werewolf, I typically howled, but here I was a second time—five months after a midnight awakening from my ghost best friend—with another ear-shattering scream.

This time, I sounded less like a child on Christmas morning and more like one of those overly dramatic voice-over shrieks in bad horror films.

After the sharp noise of breaking glass shattered through my deepest sleep, I bolted upright in bed. In my half-conscious state, I scanned the room for a shimmering ghost in a glamorous 1920s flapper girl dress.

Months earlier, I'd woken to her voice sharing good news, but Hattie wasn't here this time. No ghost hovered over me shouting *"Noema! Noema, wake up!"*

In her place was the whip of a warm summer breeze, salty and violent as it howled through the jagged glass of my broken bedroom window. I blinked at it, staring in a haze of sleep and confusion. As angry as the coastal wind was, it'd never blown hard enough to break my window before.

Flapping sounds snapped my attention to the other side of the tiny bedroom. Something darted around the shadows, dipping and swooping like a gull over the sea, except this little creature was all black and leathery.

The bat dropped down from the shadows. I instinctively ducked, but its claws still skimmed over my hair, snagging the curls I'd gathered in a bun between my wolf ears—the only feature from my wolf side that never transformed back to my human self. I tucked my wolf ears back as the bat spiraled toward me, aiming straight for my head again.

My arms flew up in a protective shell over my messy bun, and the hard bone of my elbow whacked the little intruder's belly.

The bat gave a pitiful squeak as it landed facedown on the end of my bed. My hands shot to my mouth as a gasp slipped out.

"I'm so sorry little guy!" I said.

The bat flipped over. Screeching, it fluttered pitifully up off the bed and held an erratic hover as it glared at me. I stared, unsure if the little creature would swoop at me again or was simply scared and needed help escaping the room.

A hint of ammonia stung my nose, coming from the smell of fear. My wolf ears popped up with cautious curiosity because I couldn't normally smell animals' emotions. My ability to detect feelings through scent was reserved for the deeper and more complex emotions felt by people. Maybe the ammonia was from my own fear? But I didn't usually smell myself either. Years of dealing with the scent of everyone's anger and joy, jealousy and sorrow, had made me nose blind to the smell of my own feelings.

The bat fluttered around me with an anxious energy and an even more worrisome smell. I couldn't blame the little thing for having a panic attack after smashing through a glass window and ending up trapped inside a stuffy room.

I shifted my legs to the edge of the bed and slipped my feet to the floor. With slow and gentle swoops of my arms, I swooshed at the air behind the bat to direct it toward the broken window.

The sharp tips of broken glass glinted with the shine of a near-full moon, and though the window was a hazard, the opening was plenty wide for the tiny beast to escape. Besides, guiding the poor, frightened creature through the loft, down the spiral steps, and across the video rental shop below would be impossible with its erratic and wild behavior.

The bat shot to the ceiling again and then took a dive bomb at my bun. I yelped and ducked when it came around for a second swoop. By the third pass, I caught a pattern. Each time, the bat cut and dropped, aiming first for my head and then for my bedroom door.

Its moves were no longer unpredictable, so I decided this creature must be smarter than I gave it credit for. Instead of risking the jagged window, it wanted me to open the door for a safer escape, which was the exact opposite of what I'd expected.

When the bat's wings whacked my wolf ears for a fourth time, I blew out a sigh. "All right. All right!"

I ducked and ran for the bedroom door, and as soon as I opened it, the bat shot out of my room, past my kids' room, through the kitchen and living room, and straight for the door that led to the top of the stairs. It fluttered by the door, chirping and spinning impatiently.

I promptly obeyed the angry creature as I followed and yanked open the door to the shop below. Before I could scurry to the bottom of the spiraling stairs, the bat was already swooping down into the shop and zipping to the shop door—which was also made of glass.

"Don't break it!" I squealed. Running as fast as my two legs could carry me, I bolted down the steps and past the wall of candy, the register, and several aisles stock-full of VHS tapes.

The bat only smacked its body against the glass once before I flipped the lock and threw open the door, granting the wild creature its freedom.

Except, the dang thing didn't fly off.

Instead of bursting free from the shop, the chirpy intruder made a pass at my hair again. This time, my flimsy pile of curls tumbled out of the loose bun.

"Hey," I said. "What the heck was that for? I let you out."

The bat chirped one more time before flying through the door and out into the night. I watched until the skittering black creature melted into the shadows between street lamps.

Other than the fiasco with the flying menace, Bewitcher's Beach was calm. The sound of crashing waves drifted in with the late summer breeze. The perpetual fog, even at this time of year, coated the huge park at the center of town. Ornate black iron street lamps glowed yellow in the mist.

The only bright and noisy part of our coastal town this late into the night was Roller Shakes, the twenty-four hour roller rink and diner. Shiny neon colors were as much a beacon in the darkness as the city lighthouse. A massive statue of a milkshake on wheels tilted at the top of the roller rink.

I'd been avoiding Roller Shakes, but in my half-awake state, my eyes stuck to the bright colors and my sleepy and emotional mind wandered away from me.

I blew hair out of my face as I slid my gaze away from the last place I'd seen Crow. Having a full-time traveling semi-boyfriend meant we had a part-time relationship. If we could even call it that.

Whatever it was, I missed our late-night science fiction movie dates. But even when he lived here, those were few and far between since he bounced between his Calling as a reaper of the dead and his job running Roller Shakes.

Sure, he was running all around the West Coast guiding lost spirits to rest, but that didn't mean the guy couldn't call once in a while. Hotels had phones.

My wolf ears folded back, and I refused to give Roller Shakes or its owner another thought until Crow gave me a call.

The bat still hovered in my mind. I should have thought to check him for injuries. I skimmed over the soccer field, the new baseball diamond, the walking paths, the park benches, and to the shops across town.

The little creature emerged from the shadows as a dot. It flew high and then dipped several times in front of the shops that lined the street. Briny air tossed my loose curls into my face.

I glanced down to reach for the shop door's handle, and a black rectangle caught my eye. In the middle of the cracked cobblestone sidewalk lay an abandoned VHS tape. Hair raised on the back of my neck upon me seeing the tape discarded on the ground and without its cover. The people who rented videos were getting lazier by the day.

"They couldn't even put it in the drop box?" I mumbled. I shuffled over the threshold and stooped to swipe up the tape.

The label had been peeled off. Nothing identifiable marked the tape, which meant I'd have to pop it into the VCR and watch a few minutes of the movie to figure out what it was.

A yawn overwhelmed me, cut short only by the clop of footsteps. My eyes popped open wide again and slid in the direction of the noise. Someone stood halfway between Triton's Taffy Shop and the workout studio, staring straight at me.

I could no longer spot the bat, which meant the figure in

the mist must have scared it off. That hadn't worked for me. What did this figure have that I didn't?

I got my answer immediately. They had a black cloak, a hooded face, and the ability to vanish in the split second that I dared to blink. Almost like a vampire, but as a werewolf who could shift into an animal form like a vampire changes into a bat, I knew it wasn't possible to shift and get dressed that quickly. And the bat certainly wasn't carrying clothes with it.

This figure was an unknown.

A shudder rippled through me, and goosebumps pimpled along my bare arms. I backed into the shop, pulling the door shut, all while staring at the mist. The figure was nowhere to be seen, but I didn't let myself blink again.

Not until the shop door was locked.

I dropped the VHS tape on the register so that I'd remember to watch it first thing tomorrow morning. Well, second thing tomorrow morning. The first order of business was confirming the start of construction on Everland Theater.

That first rude awakening in the wee hours of the morning five months ago had come with the wonderful news that a patron had accepted our proposal. Hattie had secured their offer to help fund the transformation of Everland Theater from the stage to the big screen.

Despite my attempt to shift my mind back to regular life, a slight shudder trickled through my neck and back.

I lingered at the register, casually glancing over my shoulder and out the windows. The figure was long gone, but my goosebumps remained. Should I call the sheriff? What could I say? That a strange person looked at me and then walked away?

Bewitcher's Beach was full of shapeshifters and vampires, and I wasn't the only werewolf. A cloaked figure wasn't actually strange at all. I was simply on high alert after the protection spell that effectively stopped attackers in their tracks was stripped away from Bewitcher's Beach. Several murders had followed, leaving the entire community shaken.

Since then, we'd had months of peace and, like most of the townspeople, I tried to settle back into the comfortable safety we'd enjoyed when magic was draped over the town.

Getting creeped out by one shadowy person didn't warrant a call to the police. It wasn't like this person was a hunter of supernatural people, nor was there a killer on the loose. The town was safe—maybe not as safe as when we had the protection spell literally stopping violence, but safer than it had been in months. Not to mention, the "police" was another man I refused to give any extra thoughts to right now.

Sett Lawrence, Bewitcher's Beach's sheriff, had almost kissed me only a few months ago—and when I had a boyfriend! Kind of had a boyfriend. Sort of. And maybe I almost wanted the kiss. Maybe I couldn't help but lean into him after he'd shown up to bail me out of jail when I was framed for murder.

Maybe I shouldn't be thinking about kissing sheriffs when I had a broken window to board up and sleep to catch up on.

I skipped up the spiral staircase, triple-locked the loft's door behind me, peeked in on my four 8-soon-to-be-9-year-olds, and then fell into bed, leaving the wind howling past the glass because it almost sounded like the howl of another werewolf. Like the family I dreamed of knowing but couldn't remember after having turned into a werewolf.

I woke to the hazy orange morning sun beaming through the jagged glass and an equally bright ghost in a dress of golden tassels.

"Rise and shine, doll," Hattie said. Her bobbed hair swished at her chin as she did a little jig to make the dress ripple. "Today's the day."

I shot up in bed almost as fast as if another bat had burst

into my room. "Today's the day!" I repeated as I hopped out from under the covers. I glanced at the clock on my nightstand glowing with green numbers.

7:00.

Construction on Everland Theater began in T-minus one hour.

In only sixty minutes, our beloved stage started its transformation to the big screen to become the first and only movie theater for miles around. The only movie theater existing in a predominantly supernatural town. The movie theater Hattie and I had dreamed of bringing to Bewitcher's Beach for years would be ready in time for the annual fall festival.

All thoughts of traveling reapers, inappropriate kisses with the sheriff, angry bats, and spooky figures in the night vanished as quickly as...the spooky figure in the night.

CHAPTER 2
HISTORY IN THE MAKING

TWO HOURS LATER, I stood beside my best friend and admired the original Everland Theater for the last time. Though we'd miss putting on stage performances for Bewitcher's Beach, Hattie and I were made for movies. She, the former Hollywood starlet from the late 1920s, and I, the aspiring screenplay writer and movie buff.

The theater towered over us with a peaked roof and a round window where the face of Hattie's daughter often peeked through. Today, the teenage ghost was nowhere to be found. Bette didn't care about the renovation, except that it distracted her overbearing mother just enough to allow her free roam to flirt with the new gargoyle boy in town.

Too bad this construction wasn't enough to distract *me* from thoughts of flirting with gargoyles. Sett Lawrence had a way of occupying my mind when he wasn't even around. In fact, since learning about a prophecy that fated me to marry a reaper, I'd avoided all interaction with Sett—sexy gargoyle sheriff or not.

Hattie elbowed me, which meant her wispy arm chilled me

like a blast of icy mist from a freezer. "Can you imagine what Rufus will say when the movie theater is finally ready?"

Rufus Harrington was the only known supernatural director in Hollywood. The half-fae man had been alive longer than Hattie haunted this world, which meant he'd been making movies since their origin. According to her, his life's goal was to bring movies to supernatural people all around the world. Since supernatural people often took to living in small towns, they didn't have access to local movie theaters and Rufus's movies had a hard time reaching their audience in the box office.

This theater would be the first to change that.

A row of glittering white teeth gleamed as she beamed at me, ever the glamorous Hollywood actress.

I grinned back at her. "He'll say he wants one of his movies to be the first on the screen."

"One of your screenplays directed by him," she said, swiping her hand through my arm again as if to give me a playful slap.

I sighed. "One step at a time. I have to finish writing it first." I'd promised my late husband I would follow this dream, but every screenplay I came close to completing didn't feel good enough. The ending wasn't coming to me. I just couldn't picture the dust settling after all the chaos. Maybe I was too used to chaos.

My gaze slid back to the theater.

The red double doors were swung wide open, propped with cement blocks. The construction crew milled in and out, removing the wood panels from the stage, old light fixtures, and outdated outlets.

The smile I'd shined at Hattie gradually dipped lower and lower. I must have been tired after my chaotic night with the bat, because witnessing the first changes to Everland Theater fell heavily over me. Like I carried the weight of each piece of wood they removed.

With every panel they marched out of the theater, another anchor tugged on my heart.

A man who reminded me of Ben Affleck—if Ben Affleck had long, dark beach waves—gestured at us from inside the theater. The contractor stood between the aisles of red-cushioned seats and held up five fingers.

Hattie gave him a thumbs up, and he mirrored it. "Meet us in five minutes at Mockbuster," she said, referring to my video rental shop next door. "Ryan wants to go over the blueprints again to verify which pieces of the original structure we're keeping."

I opened my mouth to respond, but a blond bombshell sidled up next to us on the sidewalk and interrupted.

Chanel flashed me a Baywatch-worthy smile. "Hey, gorgeous, are y'all open? I need a horror movie." The woman flicked her long hair over her shoulder, and then her blue eyes slid to Ryan. I welcomed her interruption, clearing my mind from my conflicted feelings about the changes.

Her thick eyelashes dropped.

Did I see a wink? As a siren, Chanel had a way with her appearance. To the untrained eye, she looked like a naturally stunning human, not a supernatural siren woman with the ability to drop men to their knees with a single look.

Ryan didn't return her attention, but several other men did. Triton, the taffy shop owner, stopped his morning walk long enough to gawk at Chanel. For him, this was a regular occurrence, but he was joined by a hairy man with a wild, thick beard from the construction crew and the new baseball coach in town, who was whacking a ball with a steel bat at the mound across the street.

Chanel ignored every one of them, though they seemed to

pull toward her magnetic energy. It was a little unsettling how they stared for so long when she'd only intended to draw Ryan's attention. Or maybe my wolf senses were too tapped in after last night. Chanel probably got this kind of attention all the time, and it clearly didn't bother her.

I was the one who didn't like being watched. Give me a simple task like drinking out of a straw, then put me in front of an audience, and I'd end up with the straw stuck in my nose and Diet Pepsi spurting out one nostril.

I turned to her. "Are you sure you want a horror movie? It might scare your kiddos." I'd never normally question anyone's preference, but I knew Chanel's movie renting habits well enough to know she'd never once selected a horror film. She was all about the romcoms and raunchy flicks.

"My boys are at summer camp with your lot," she said.

"Oh! Fun. Dio has been wanting to teach them soccer. He says your little guys are both kickers." My son was obsessed with sports.

She blew out a breath. "Good, I need something to keep them busy so I can get back in the dating scene." She pushed out her plush lips, eyes darting back to Ryan. "Anyway, horror movies are perfect for dates."

"Are they?" I glanced at Ryan.

"Absolutely. Haven't you heard that men love it when their date gets a little scared and clings to them?" She fanned herself as if the morning breeze wasn't enough.

"Scared? Hmm, how about a summer slasher? I have the perfect recommendation."

"Sure." She shrugged and trailed me next door, her heels clicking against the cobblestone.

Inside Mockbuster, I plucked *I Know What You Did Last Summer* off the rack and handed it to her. There was nothing scarier than watching someone who looked similar to you get stalked by a killer, and Chanel was a dead ringer for Sarah Michelle Gellar.

I walked to the desk with the register, staring at the blank tape I'd left there last night. Sometime between working at the shop, overseeing the construction, and herding the kids home from summer camp, I'd have to squeeze in a moment to identify the movie and create a new label.

Chanel paid for the rental, but she lingered at the register, batting her eyelashes when Ryan walked in. Hattie followed close behind. They crowded around the register, ready for the meeting, when Chanel spoke up.

"Hey," she said in a velvet voice. She laid a manicured hand on Ryan's forearm and held up the tape with the other. "Have you ever seen this?"

He furrowed his brow and shook his head before gently sliding away from her touch. Chanel's Barbie-pink lips twisted, but only for a moment.

"I thought you might like to watch it with me," she said. He only glanced at her, but it didn't deter her confidence. "Don't you remember me? We chatted at the bar at The Oyster Inn? You said you love a good horror film?"

He offered her a weak smile. "Sure, yeah. We were making conversation."

Whatever flirtatious power Chanel tried to cast on Ryan wasn't working, but she still pursued him.

"So what do you say?" she continued. "We can watch it together over another Bordeaux?"

Ryan pulled his long, wavy locks to the back of his head and held a smile like a mask on his face. If Chanel's blond hair and toned frame gave her a Sarah Michelle Gellar look, Ryan's thick hair and 5'10" body gave him a Noema Wolf look.

If I had a brother, did he look like Ryan?

I gave myself a little shake. Ever since I got a clue that could lead to my family, thoughts like this had seeped into my daily routine. In reality, Ryan and I looked nothing alike beyond the height and hair.

Besides, thanks to an uncovered prophecy, I knew I belonged to a family of witches, and Ryan had said he'd never been around so many supernaturals when he first came to Bewitcher's Beach. He definitely did not come from a witchy lineage.

"No, thank you," Ryan finally said as Chanel inched closer to him. "Now, if you don't mind, I'm here to discuss work." When he turned away from her, she huffed and straightened, pushing her chest against his arm.

"Work huh?" She looked at him, but he didn't give her any more attention. "You won't be working any longer if that lawsuit wins." Leaning closer to him, she nearly whispered, but my wolf ears caught every word. "I heard about your company dumping in a lake."

Ryan finally slid his gaze to her. "That case is closed, and I fired the guys who did that."

Whatever he was talking about, it was the truth. I got a reprieve from her odorous irritation when the scent of Ryan's truth filled the air with lavender and sandalwood-smelling confidence.

He shuffled away from her and then winced. I gathered that she must have jammed her heel into his foot as she stormed past him.

"Not all of them," she muttered as she marched off. The smoky scent of her anger faded with her footsteps.

Ryan glanced between Hattie and me. "I didn't mean to be rude to your friend, but I already told her I'm taken when she talked to me at the bar," he said. Glancing outside, a small smile lifted his face. "I'm actually thinking of bringing my girlfriend to this beach to propose soon."

Hattie and I released a chorus of "awes" before we dove into the blueprints, neither of us too worried about Chanel, considering she marched right out of the shop and started chatting up a very red-faced baseball coach. He attempted to toss a ball up and down and catch it as he trailed her back across town.

The three of us argued over whether to recarpet the theater or uncover the original flooring from 1933. When Hattie first haunted Everland Theater, she covered all remnants of the Art Deco style from the 1930s, including the mosaic black and gold jagged tiles. Now her preference switched. She missed the style of the past, but Ryan and I argued for the benefits of the sound acoustics. Carpet was the ideal choice.

The bell above the door chimed as the shop's door flew open and the burning smell of anger drifted back in. I gritted my molars, suddenly worried the glass door would shatter after last night's broken window.

A stout woman with a man's haircut stomped over to us and jammed a finger toward the door. The scales of her half-dragon heritage shimmered under her skin only when the light hit her just right. "Are you the owners of The Grand Regent?"

"Everland Theater," Hattie corrected without a beat.

"The Grand Regent," the woman said, nearly stamping her foot like a frustrated toddler. "That is the original name for the theater built here before Bewitcher's Beach was even an established town. The Grand Regent shall remain. It's already an abomination to the preservationists that you've dared remove the original oak paneling from the stage."

My heart flipped. Our dream was on the horizon, but with

this intrusion, the horizon suddenly felt miles away. I didn't know how I felt about it, but Hattie's reaction was obvious from her sour frown.

She looked ready to surge forward and haunt this half-dragon's scales right off, but she only folded her arms. "I've owned Everland Theater for decades, and while we aim to keep much of it the same"—she shot a daggered glance at me and Ryan—"the stage will be renovated to a movie screen, and that's final."

The woman fumbled with her cloth purse and yanked out a business card, shoving it into our faces. "I'm Olivia Woodstone, the president of the official West Coast Historic Preservationist Society. If you dare touch one more of those wood planks, I'll turn your life into a nightmare."

My pulse jumped. I'd already been awake most of the night thanks to a certain bat breaking into both my room and my dreams. Daytime didn't need to come with nightmares, too.

This time, Hattie surged forward, coming nose-to-nose with Ms. Woodstone. "You'll have to go through me first."

Olivia only laughed. "Poor choice of words. You're aware that you're a ghost, and that I can step right through you?"

"Go ahead and try it," Hattie dared. "Half-dragons hate to be cold. And for the official West Coast Historic Preser-whatever Society's information, when I purchased that theater, I squared away all my rights to renovate it legally. Good luck."

Olivia only smirked. Without another word, she spun around and marched out the door toward the theater.

We exchanged glances before rushing outside after her. Sure enough, the historic society's president was already screaming at the construction crew that they'd each be sued.

The beefy man with the buzzcut scratched his head while the other crew members shrank away from the barking historian.

In a town as tight and small as Bewitcher's Beach, Ms.

Woodstone's temper tantrum became a stage of its own. The baseball coach gawked, Mae and Wallace stopped their morning walk to eavesdrop, and Barney emerged from The Oyster Inn across the alley from Everland Theater.

And after only a few moments, a massive gargoyle clad in a navy blue uniform came striding up to us.

I sucked in a sharp breath and snapped my eyes away from Sett. Averting my gaze from him was a habit now, because if I thought of him too much—of how he'd been there for me when no one else was—that little ache at the center of my chest would crop up again, and I'd find myself at the bottom of a carton of Ben and Jerry's Chunky Monkey ice cream.

Thoughts of Sett while I was dating Crow were inappropriate at best and painful at worst. Not only that, according to my family's prophecy, I was fated to marry Crow—or more vaguely, a reaper. But I had no doubt it was Crow. Crow and I were one and the same: spontaneous, science-fiction-loving free spirits with a penchant for thrill seeking.

Sett was safe, with a slow lifestyle, and he was like...*home*.

I shook my head.

No, I'd never had a home that I could remember. Not since Christopher passed away. My late husband was the only home I'd ever really known. Bewitcher's Beach came close, but to me, the people we loved were the true home. And a nearly seven-foot grumpy gargoyle was definitely not home for a wild werewolf.

Sett calmed Olivia down long enough for us to speak with her.

"What if we use the stage's original wood paneling along the walls?" I suggested. Olivia's mouth twitched, but it wasn't a frown, so I kept going. "We can also style the theater with nods to the original 1930s Art Deco. Adding some gold and black with bold, jagged prints?" I looked between Hattie, Ryan, and Olivia.

Hattie and Ryan nodded, but Olivia's fist crumpled over her business card. Despite her white knuckles, her voice was pleasant. "I'd like to see the plans for that to verify it does The Grand Regent honor."

We all nodded like a gang of bobble-head toys. Why the small crowd of onlookers still hung around, I didn't know. Discussing the theater's renovation wasn't exactly riveting now that the screaming had ceased.

Olivia looked suspicious, but Ryan offered a suggestion that softened her scowl. "We'll go over it tonight and have the plans ready for you tomorrow."

"Let's meet at my loft," I said to Ryan and Hattie. "It's just me tonight; the kids are at a sleepover." They shot me two thumbs up. Still holding their thumbs in the air, our attention shifted to Olivia.

A tense minute passed before she rolled her eyes. "Fine, but if I don't see those plans first thing tomorrow morning, you should watch your backs." Her eyes fixed on me as if I'd personally offended her. Maybe Hattie had scared her enough that she took her anger out on me.

A shiver bolted through me.

Sett stepped between us, a veritable wall of stone-like skin. "That's enough. You cannot threaten the crew or the owners." Olivia only huffed and spun away.

Once again, Sett had come to my rescue. Of course, it *was* his job.

He turned to face me, forcing me to acknowledge him with a watery smile. "I'll keep an eye out for you until this blows over," he said.

"No thanks," I said, too quickly. The more time I spent around him, the closer I'd come to slipping up about the prophecy. I couldn't pinpoint why I nearly hurled at the thought of telling him my fate was bound to a reaper. Apparently, the taste of bile made me irritable.

He straightened, slightly pulling away as if I'd slapped him. "But I always—"

"Well don't!" I snapped.

I ducked past him and hurried back into Mockbuster before his presence pulled me in like Chanel's magnetic force. Something about that almost-kiss left me feeling like a schoolgirl with a crush, so I hid away in the shop where I was busy with a steady flow of customers for the rest of the day.

I didn't get a break until nightfall, when the townspeople were finally settled at home watching their rentals, including my kids. They'd gathered at Mae and Wallace's house—friends of mine who basically adopted my lot as their grandchildren— to watch *Lion King* for the hundredth time.

With the shop quiet, I turned to a shelf behind the register. Black wires hung down, connecting a VCR to the TV I'd had Sett mount on the wall. The TV looped new releases for promotional purposes, but today, I didn't have enough time to pick a movie and turn it on.

I slid the blank tape in, hoping it would take my mind off the stress. The old VCR whirred as it took its sweet time getting started while worry about the legal standing of Everland Theater needled me.

We'd finally witnessed the change that'd lead to our movie theater dreams, only to come up against a historical barrier. And I didn't even know if this *comforted* me or not. What the heck was wrong with me?

Lack of sleep turned everything into a nightmare as my brain obsessed over how the past kept coming back to haunt me.

The historic origin of Everland Theater.

The old prophecy that I must marry a reaper.

Sett's inappropriate almost-kiss.

The fact that I knew nothing about my family because I'd become a werewolf.

I'd searched for my identity from before turning into a werewolf, but I remembered nothing and found very little. Only a few months ago did I learn that I'd been a witch who applied to attend Shadowvale University. The past haunted me then too. Though I'd recovered bits and pieces of my memory from when I visited Shadowvale as a teenager, I'd also found out that someone tried to frame me for the murder of the university's dean.

The cold case had led nowhere. I told Sett to drop it because I couldn't bear to spend much time around him. Besides, the peace in Bewitcher's Beach became an addiction. As much as I wanted to know my identity and the family I grew up with, I relished the simplicity of these quiet months here at Mockbuster.

No murders, no unsettling prophecies, no *changes*.

Something slammed into the glass door, and I startled from my hazy stare at the woman who'd finally popped up on the screen.

A bat smacked its body at the door over and over again, and though I swore the woman in the movie said my name, I abandoned the TV and ran for the door before the bat broke the glass.

I yanked open the door, and it zipped inside, screeching wildly as it flapped around my head in a frenzy.

Before I knew what'd hit me, the bat darted for my arm and sank its sharp little teeth into my flesh. Hot pain cut through my forearm, and a shriek escaped me. The bat fluttered back and snapped its jaws around my bicep and then bit my hand, relentless in its attack.

A voice drifted from the still-playing video on the TV screen. "This is a warning..."

My head swayed as blood beaded to the surface of my skin, and only one thought swirled around as relentlessly as the bat.

The past had literally come back to bite me, again, and again, and again.

CHAPTER 3
THREE'S A CROWD

THE ROOM SPUN AROUND ME, along with the snapping bat. Blood didn't normally bother me, but that, coupled with the pain and the dizzying effect of flapping wings in my face, made my head feel like it'd float off my shoulders.

The bat's tiny teeth sank deep into my skin, and it seemed to try to pull me out the door as it tugged on my arm.

Swatting it off of me, I leaned against the door frame and slowly sank to my knees. The bat screeched and screeched and screeched, a piercing sound that bolted through my temples like lightning. I gently laid my palm over the first bite. None of the bites were deep, but they continued to bleed.

What did this crazy creature want from me? I thought vampire bats quietly sucked a person's blood and then zipped away. This menace wasn't even drinking from me, just chomping away like he was at a picnic and my arm was his corn on the cob.

Shock and confusion muted the stinging, but the spinning in my head didn't slow down. Bewitcher's Beach became a faded background of brown and green swirls.

The screeching finally ceased, and the bat flew off at the

approach of footsteps. Growing louder, the stomping feet barreled toward me in a breakout run. I dragged my head up to see a figure in all black, with the moon's bright light beaming behind them.

A defensive growl rumbled from me until my eyes adjusted and their face filled in. Midnight black curls hung over a pale face with sharp cheekbones and a striking jawline. An old scar cut from his mouth across his cheek.

"Crow?" I mumbled. My brain hadn't accepted that he was actually here. He wasn't supposed to return from his trip for another two weeks, and even that wasn't confirmed.

He dropped to his knees in front of me, cupping my uninjured arm. His heavy breathing made his chest heave beneath his tight black T-shirt. "You're hurt."

I blinked up at him as he inspected my bloody arm.

"A bat bit me," I said, my voice faint and floaty.

"I know, I saw it fly off," he said. "I ran as fast as I could once I saw you were in trouble. We need to get you to the clinic right now."

"But I have a meeting." I waved my hand lazily toward the inside of Mockbuster. In less than an hour, Hattie and Ryan expected me to host them at the loft.

When Crow shook his head, curls fell into his face. "Not anymore." He gently slipped his arm beneath both of mine and helped me to my feet.

I tried to turn back to the door. "I need to close down the store."

"I'll get the lights." He steadied me where I could lean against the wall, one hand splayed out on the glass windows. Ducking inside, he shouted. "I'll lock up. Where are your keys?"

I opened my mouth, but I only managed to shake my head. I was sinking again.

Crow bolted outside, letting the door fall shut behind him, but someone beat him to me. Two strong arms scooped me up.

"What are you doing?" Crow snapped.

"Carrying her." My rescuer's chest vibrated with his low voice. *Sett.* I gritted my teeth.

"I see that." Crow's voice again. Everything was hazy, like the mist that clung to the ground each night had fogged up my brain. "She needs Doctor Pitt, not the sheriff."

"That's where I'm going," Sett said.

I twisted to peek past his bicep at the shop. The Open sign was flicked off, along with all the overhead lights. Thankfully, the register was already emptied and closed out. Maybe Hattie would tell Ryan to come inside and show him upstairs, and I could catch up on the discussion after getting bandaged.

"Don't you have a crime to solve or something?" Crow's voice was rough. Sett only chuckled, knowing this would trigger Crow. "I can take Noema to the clinic."

"You were too slow," Sett said. I almost laughed. That was rich coming from the most methodical and frustratingly slow person I'd ever met. Sett did and said nothing without first thinking it over a dozen times. At least this detail orientation made him a good detective and an even better chef.

"I was doing what she asked." Crow said. "Did she ask you to carry her?"

Sett peeked down at me, a near-smile ghosting over his lips. He was enjoying irritating Crow far too much, and it was probably my fault. If I hadn't complained to Mae, and Hattie, and Bette, and anyone else who'd listen that I didn't like how often Crow was gone, Sett wouldn't have caught wind of it. I knew him well enough to know this was his way of sending Crow a message.

"Do you want me to put you down?" he asked.

My stomach flipped because I didn't want that. All I really

wanted was a crisp Diet Pepsi and a good night's sleep, not to be caught between this verbal brawl. But his arms were safe, and we were already on our way to the clinic.

Since I said nothing, Sett smirked until the salty breeze cut through my many open wounds, and I seethed, wiping his cocky grin away.

With concern glittering in his gray eyes and a crease between his brows, his gaze darted from me to the street. Sett Lawrence, the slowest moving person on planet Earth, picked up the pace even more. In a few steps, we were at the door to the clinic.

Crow opened it, and Sett stepped inside, marching me straight to the bed in the open exam room.

Doctor Pitt's assistant hopped up from behind the front desk and called for her boss. As Doctor Pitt appeared and made quick work of assessing, cleaning, and bandaging the bites, Crow shot Sett a side-eye glance. I ignored it, focusing on answering Doctor Pitt's questions.

Yes, I knew what bit me; it was a bat. No, I didn't think the bat looked sick. Yes, it behaved aggressively. No, I'd never had a rabies shot. Yes, I absolutely wanted one.

With the questions complete, I tuned in to the tension between the two men still hovering in the exam room.

"I've got it from here," Crow said, still glaring at Sett. Smoky irritation burned in my nose.

Sett ignored him, eyes on me. "What happened?" he asked.

Crow jumped in before I could respond. "Didn't you hear? A bat bit her, not a criminal, so you're not needed here."

Sett's jaw flexed as he finally turned to Crow. "At least I *am* here."

Crow's eyes narrowed. "What's that supposed to mean?"

"You got lucky you showed up just in time tonight, but you weren't around when she got arrested at Shadowvale, or when she needed help mounting a TV on the wall. She doesn't like—"

"Sett!" I snapped before he spilled my can of complaints labeled *Crow*. "Thank you for carrying me here, but I specifically asked you not to keep an eye on me."

He folded his arms and set his jaw. "But you'll tell me if you need anything?"

"Yes."

"Animal control? Anything?"

I suppressed a sudden smile. *Animal Control* had become a bit of an inside joke between us since I'd visited Shadowvale University and discovered that my daughter did, in fact, have a special ability to communicate with animals. As much as I'd avoided Sett lately, I couldn't take him away from my children. He played soccer with Dio, snuck books from the library for Jovi, fixed Halen's camcorder, and nicknamed Stevie *Animal Control*.

I swallowed the smile and nodded. "I'll be fine."

Sett hesitated for a moment, our eyes locked on one another. While Doctor Pitt worked on my injured arm, I lifted my free hand and tapped my lips. This was another little joke we shared about how I often said I was speechless and then continued to ramble. He was speechless now, but the small gesture seemed to relax him.

The tension in his shoulders dropped, and he nodded. "I'll leave you to it then." Without acknowledging Crow, he ducked out of the exam room.

My semi-boyfriend sat in the visitor's chair beside the bed and laid his palm on my shoulder. The thin white paper covering the exam bed stuck to the back of my legs. I usually preferred to wear a band T-shirt and jeans, but humidity hit an all-time high this summer, so I'd opted for jean shorts today.

After Doctor Pitt had worked his magic, which was the

magic of modern medicine, sterilization, bandaging, and a rabies shot, he left with an invitation welcoming us to stay and rest here as long as I needed.

I lay my head back against the bed and stared up at the ceiling. "I'm sorry about Sett," I said.

"He was right." Crow's tight voice had me rolling my head to the side. I blinked at him. "I haven't been here for you."

"Your Calling is important."

"You're important too," he said. "And I'm here tonight. That last spirit the other reapers had me help with had an easy passage, so I came back as early as possible. Besides, *Armageddon* is out of theaters now, right? We can have a popcorn and sci-fi night?"

His striking dark eyes and crooked grin sent my pulse skipping. There was no doubt Crow was handsome, but my thumping heart dipped. He was here tonight, and maybe tomorrow, but how much longer?

I returned a tight smile as he helped me off the bed. "Let's do it," I said, already looking forward to the popcorn. "As long as that bat doesn't come back."

"It better not," he said as I followed him out of the exam room. He opened the door, and I stepped outside. "I had no idea Bewitcher's Beach had an animal control department."

"Oh," I said, eyes avoiding the police department to the right. "It doesn't."

"No kidding? Then who will take care of the bat?"

"Stevie could," I said. "She's been practicing communicating with wild animals, both magical and ordinary. She found a frog with the ability to predict when it will rain."

"No kidding?" He repeated. "That's right, I forgot Bewitcher's Beach used to have a lot of wild animals with magical tendencies, right?"

"It still does. I think they've just now started to come out of hiding."

The bat crossed my mind again. Did it have any special abilities? It'd come to me twice now, and since it didn't bite me the first time, maybe I'd missed its message. The bite could have been a threat or a warning of something else.

Tomorrow, I'd ask Stevie to give me tips on how to understand bat screeches in case it came back a third time.

CHAPTER 4
FACE DOWN

THE TREK back to Mockbuster was an agonizing snail's pace.

I had downed enough juice at the clinic that the world had stopped spinning, but my head still felt like a balloon ready to float up into the night sky. Sensing this, Crow shuffled alongside me, gingerly touching my back to support my balance. Even without the faintness, my coordination on two feet was dismal.

So, we took the slowest walk through town I'd ever experienced.

"You're quiet," Crow said.

That was new; I was rarely quiet. At least without careful intent, and usually only when I listened to a suspect.

"Is your arm hurting?" he asked.

"Not anymore," I said. "I'm just...tired."

He nodded and we shuffled along in silence. We had heaps to talk about after weeks apart, but I didn't know where to start and this floating feeling carried my focus away from him. My gaze flitted over the dog groomers, the hair salon, and The Oyster Inn.

For the first time, I noticed most shops and houses left their windows open wide for the summer breeze to blow through. More cars than usual were parked along the cobblestone street from the influx of visitors. Though it was busier than any summer before, a sense of safety blanketed the town like mist.

Peace had gradually changed Bewitcher's Beach back to the comfortable, easy place it'd been in the past.

I should have rejoiced, but the subtle changes set my canines on edge. Gritting my teeth, I stared too long at the visitors milling in and out of The Oyster Inn. There were so many of them, and they laughed and chatted loud enough that if my kids were home, they'd have been woken late in the night. Plus, with the influx of people, I couldn't help but worry about crime rates going up, or even a rare hunter slipping in. After meeting a hunter at Shadowvale only a few months ago, they'd been on my mind.

The increasing number of visitors and new move-ins also had the grocer placing orders large enough that brought a semi-truck into town once a week. The ugly rectangular box with *Delivered Fresh!* splashed on the side blocked my view of Mockbuster.

I swallowed the growl rumbling up my throat.

More people meant more patrons for Everland Theater—or rather, Everland Movie Theater. Dang, that sounded like a dream come true. So why did it flip my stomach inside out? I bared my teeth at every subtle change that suddenly felt like it'd stripped away the Bewitcher's Beach I'd grown used to this last year.

The protection spell wasn't back, but the hints of the former times slipped into every crack and corner, and I was probably the only soul in the entire town who didn't want to celebrate this.

Even the magical animals coming out of hiding knew these

changes were welcoming. Warm. But I was a werewolf. I hated too much warmth. And, apparently, change.

I'd spent years stuck on my screenplays because none of them were good enough for the promise I'd made to my husband.

I'd spent years wondering about and searching for the family I'd lost only to find out that being part of my family meant I didn't have the option to marry whomever I wanted.

I'd spent years dreaming of bringing a movie theater to Bewitcher's Beach, only for an angry historian to almost bring it down in a single day.

A shiver zipped down my spine.

Mistaking my shaking for cold, Crow pulled me closer to him, hooking his arm around my shoulders to keep me warm beside him. He must have forgotten werewolves rarely get cold. It took the icy spirit of a ghost or the persistent wetness of winter to chill me.

I offered him a watery smile as we stepped into the shadow of the semi-truck blocking Mockbuster. Darkness shrouded the shop. We crossed the cobblestone, and Crow hurried to step ahead of me, reaching for Mockbuster's door. Pulling it open, he waved for me to pass through first.

I stepped up to the threshold when I spotted a lump sprawled on the carpet in the shadows. I froze as my eyes adjusted to the darkness.

Lying face down in the middle of Mockbuster was a man in scuffed boots and thick denim work pants. The back of his T-shirt showed the logo for Level Head Construction Co. with a silhouette of a person's head and a yellow level tool slashed across the shape. The man's long, wavy hair, which usually covered his shirt, was splayed out like a spread mop, and blood darkened the back of his head. On the ground beside him was my VCR, discarded like a piece of broken trash.

Crow peered over my shoulder. "Who is that?"

"Ryan," I said. "The contractor we hired for Everland Theater."

"Somebody..."

"Killed him," I finished for him. That much was obvious. Somebody had whacked the VCR against Ryan's skull. Except, the stain of red beneath his neck didn't come from the blood on his head. At least we knew it wasn't a hunter. Hunters came prepared with guns; they didn't reach for the nearest object— like a VCR—to end their victims.

I narrowed my eyes and floated closer, my entire body suddenly a piece of the background as I zeroed in on the strange spread of blood.

"What is it?" Crow asked, his voice a hollow echo in my wake. As a reaper, he was no stranger to death, but my lack of focus on him and his questions painted him as part of the fading world around me.

"The blood..." I pointed at Ryan's neck. Shuffling closer, I sank to my knees. The rough carpet scratched against my skin.

Droplets of red dotted the gray carpet from two sunken holes along the side of his throat. They looked like two punctures into clay, with his skin so pale and not so much as a scab forming over them. Had the bat returned? No, if I remembered my bites correctly, they were far smaller than this. This came from a vampire in their true form, though I supposed the bat could have been a vampire.

Blood beaded at the punctures. His bleeding was slow, having dripped only a couple of times since the bite. Maybe the vampire had almost bled him dry.

My gaze flicked from the VCR to the bite, back to the VCR, and then to the shiny wet blood on his skull.

"This is weird," I mumbled. I glanced at Crow, who was scanning the entire room. He didn't move a muscle except for his eyes. He didn't blink. He probably didn't even breathe. Finally, his gaze landed on Ryan's back. "What is it?" I echoed his question from earlier.

His cheek twitched, dark eyes dropping to two miniscule slits. After a tense two seconds, he released a puff of air. "This guy's spirit is already laid to rest."

"You were assessing him?" I asked.

He nodded, pushing curls away from his forehead with the heel of his palm. A sheen of sweat caught in the weak glow of the single security light hanging over Mockbuster's back door. "I can pinpoint if a spirit is lingering a lot faster than I used to, but it still takes a hell of a lot of focus." He pinched his temples with his thumb and forefinger and slowly massaged them.

I looked back at Ryan, sudden tears welling in my eyes. "He was going to propose to his girlfriend. Something like that wouldn't keep his spirit here long enough to turn into a ghost?"

Crow sighed. "No. He was likely settled in all his decisions. Full of love rather than unrest."

I nodded. "I suppose that's a good thing. But his poor girl-friend." I knew exactly how she was about to feel. Well, not exactly. Christopher wasn't murdered.

"Murdered," I breathed. *At Mockbuster.* Again.

This was the second homicidal incident near my rental shop. Last time, a man had been poisoned and dropped dead at the front step with a handful of video tapes. Then, everyone had feared it was my fault, believing that I *cursed* my customers.

Now, it really was my fault. Well, maybe not the murder itself, but if I hadn't run off and left the shop unlocked, maybe Ryan would still be alive. Maybe the killer needed the VCR to whack him with and finish the job after attacking him.

But what vampire would do this? All the vampires I knew drank synthetic blood. None of them cared for this barbaric behavior when tastier, healthier, humane options were available in most grocery stores.

The grocer next door stocked a whole aisle of YumBlood from birthday cake flavor to Bloody Marys, complete with a splash of vodka if the vampire wanted to party.

"Is that a crucifix?" Crow asked.

I snapped my attention to where he pointed. Ryan's limp fist was still loosely curled around a silver necklace. The cross pendant wasn't one I'd seen him wear around his neck before. Maybe he'd kept the jewelry in his pocket or couldn't wear it while at the construction site.

"And he has..." I tipped forward, noting the earthy musk of raw garlic. I sniffed along his body, stopping at his jean pockets. "Garlic in his pockets, too."

"So he knew a vampire was after him."

Like the vampire bat that was after me? A convulsion bolted through my shoulders, and I willed myself not to keep shivering.

"But why wait until he was going to a meeting—" I popped upright. "Where's Hattie?" Maybe she'd witnessed the murder and was already on her way to the police station to tell Sett what she'd seen. Was Olivia Woodstone actually a vampire? The historian had been so angry, *and* she knew about the time and location of our meeting tonight. She may have thought ending Ryan's life would stop the renovation of Everland Theater while also providing her with a snack.

Modern vampires were tricky to identify, thanks to sunscreen and UV-blocking fabrics that allowed them to go out during the day. But I didn't notice her fangs.

If Olivia attacked Ryan, she may have gone for Hattie too. Ghosts weren't easy to destroy, but they weren't impossible either. With the correct blade, she could slash through a spirit and end their existence, but that was rare.

I blinked up at Crow. "We need to call Sett." My voice came out shaky. "And we need to find Hattie."

He nodded and rushed to the phone on the wall behind the register. Everything other than the VCR was where it belonged. None of the racks of video tapes were knocked over. The shelf where the VCR had been was still intact, and there were no signs of struggle. If Olivia whacked Ryan, she must have taken him by surprise.

She didn't play with her food. It was hit first, then she dined.

This happening at the same time as the vampire bat's attack couldn't be a coincidence. Could the bat that bit me have been Olivia hiding her true form? The creature came for me the day of the construction and then returned for Ryan. Plus, the bat was no ordinary animal, not with that strength and intelligence. With the way it communicated, it was either magical or a vampire.

Maybe Olivia had gone easier on me because I was the one who suggested we keep much of the original style from the Grand Regent.

Or would the bat have managed to kill me if Crow and Sett hadn't shown up?

CHAPTER 5
EVIDENCE

OVERHEAD LIGHTS FLOODED Mockbuster in a wash of stark white that felt too bright for the somber scene. My contractor lay dead in the middle of my shop, and my best friend was being questioned about his murder.

Hattie's glare could have drilled holes through Sett's stony skull. She folded her thin arms over the front of her dress and pursed her lips, drawing her tight cheekbones sharper. Crow shuffled from my side to stand with Hattie. He folded his arms and glared at Sett as if he and Hattie were an opposing team playing a silent game against the sheriff. A mild whiff of his smoky irritation prickled my nose. Apparently, Crow was still bitter about Sett's obnoxious comments. I fought the urge to roll my eyes. Sett had crossed a line, but what he'd said was entirely true and Crow had yet to acknowledge that.

I sat slumped in the stool behind Mockbuster's register, my wolf ears tuned into the investigation as my gaze flicked between the three of them.

"What time was it that you said you saw Mr. Belleville?" Sett asked, using Ryan's last name to offer respect to the victim.

"Half past ten," Hattie said with a huff. "I told him to tell

Noema that I'd be late to the meeting because I had to find Bette. Sure enough, she was off running around with that hoodlum who moved in down the street. It doesn't matter how many times I tell her that ghost girls don't date, she still sneaks out to flirt with boys." Hattie's voice rose higher and more shrill with every word. Tucking my wolf ears back now, I protected them from her inevitable outburst. If Hattie was anything, she was a protective mom. Some would say overprotective. Whenever Bette stole glances with a young man, Hattie haunted the daylights out of the poor boy.

Crow laid a hand on Hattie's shoulder. As a trained reaper now, he could interact more easily with ghosts and spirits than anyone else. This support only seemed to fuel Hattie. Her spine straightened, and she jabbed a finger at Sett's face. "Why haven't you ever taken my suggestion for a curfew for teenagers? If you see them out past ten, you can arrest them because with a curfew, they'd be breaking the law."

Sett stopped scribbling notes and raised his palm to calm her. Ignoring him, Hattie descended into a shrieking tangent.

"Do you want to know the worst part of this whole night? I found out that Bette wanted to learn how to solidify her body so that she could kiss him. And they did! I saw them necking with my own eyes." She wagged a glowing finger in his face. "You should be patrolling The Gull, not standing around here doing nothing."

Sett pinched the bridge of his nose and shook his head.

"What?" Hattie demanded. "Doesn't the sheriff know about The Gull? It's an outcropping of rock shadowed by the lighthouse where all the kids go to smooch."

He released a sigh, his shoulders dropping with the long exhale. "You're hovering over a man's dead body, Hattie. It's tactless to say a couple of teens hanging out requires more attention than this."

She paled, suddenly coming down from her high temper. The wispy frame of her body followed suit, slowly drifting closer to the ground until her transparent feet stood on the carpet. Her throat tensed as she cleared away imaginary phlegm.

"I suppose you're not wrong," she said. She straightened the glittering feather headband around her forehead. "Ryan deserves better. All I can tell you is that I saw him headed toward Mockbuster at about ten thirty. It seemed we were both a little late since that's when we were supposed to be at the shop. We crossed paths outside of Roller Shakes. I believe he'd just eaten since he was carrying a paper cup from the diner inside. I went there hoping Bette learned to solidify so that she could roller skate." Her chin quivered, and Crow's open palm rubbed soothing circles at the top of Hattie's back. "My poor, stupid, innocent baby girl. If she takes after me, she'll end up partying with the worst of them."

Bette was eighteen when she became a ghost, and she'd existed for a total of 55 years now. Even if she acted like a teenager at times, she wasn't the baby girl Hattie believed her to be. Besides, she didn't even have the opportunity to rub elbows with mobsters in illegal speakeasies. Bewitcher's Beach wasn't 1920s Hollywood.

"Did you see anyone with Mr. Belleville? Maybe someone watching him in or around Roller Shakes?" Sett asked.

Hattie's perfect complexion was only creased by a tiny wrinkle between her brows. It vanished after a moment. "Yes." She nodded. "I remember spotting someone in a maroon and black cloak. I remember because they were walking outside of Everland Theater and, at first, I thought maybe they'd climbed the construction fences to break into our costume stock in the attic. We have a few cloaks lying around up there, you see, but really nothing as fancy as their silk and velvet. So I left them alone."

The figure from the night of the bat popped into my mind. Hadn't they been wearing a cloak? I dug one of my canines into my bottom lip and chewed thoughtfully. It'd been impossible to see the color of the figure's clothing that night.

I mulled over the facts before my mind ran away with cliched ideas.

A vampire bat attacked me.

The bat had only disappeared when the figure appeared.

That same figure was spotted near here around the time of Ryan's death.

And he'd been bitten by a vampire.

Okay, so the facts themselves were cliche enough. Modern vampires didn't even wear cloaks, as far as I knew. One of the servers at Roller Shakes was a vampire, and she dressed more fashionably than most humans. I'd never once seen Cordelia in a cloak.

And even though vampires could learn to turn into bats, most never bothered to try—at least, that was what she'd told me when we were discussing how my clothes always fell off when I shifted into my werewolf form. I'd asked her for advice on how she keeps her nice skirts and blouses clean when she transforms only to find out that, like most vampires, she never learned to transform.

The bell above Mockbuster's door chimed. Bartholomew Martin the Third, Bewitcher's Beach's town coroner, stepped inside. His sparse white hair and bulging eyes made him look more like the stereotypical mad scientist than the friendly, partially-retired coroner. He'd only picked up work again when the protection spell was stripped away and murders occurred in the town he'd chosen for his retirement.

His appearance had aged about twenty years since the first

murder here less than a year ago. And maybe it was lack of sleep, but tonight, his static-spread strands and hurried shuffle further pinned him as a mad scientist.

"Bart," Sett said with a kind nod. "Thank you for coming down."

Bart gave him a pitiful smile. He crouched over the victim, his bugged eyes nearly ready to pop out of his head and roll across the crime scene. Murder had never shaken Bart before, but the smell of ammonia confirmed his fear.

I couldn't exactly blame him. After several months of peace, we'd all grown too comfortable. Another murder would unsettle even the most stoic, especially considering that it happened where all this started, like a reminder of the day we discovered the protection spell we all believed in had both been real and stolen.

The only person who wanted to take away a protection spell was a person who wanted to hurt us, and we'd never found out who would—or even could—strip away the magic.

After a few moments of huffing breaths and creaking knees, Bart stood up and peeled off his rubber gloves with a snap. "Yep. Someone drained him."

"A vampire?" Sett asked, his brow heavy over his gray eyes.

Bart shrugged. "Who else? I never heard of no ghost or reaper or wolf who drinks blood." He nodded at each of us, his lips flat and his red nose sniffling.

"What about the VCR?" I asked as my gaze fell to the black box that held the mysterious videotape. In all the chaos, I'd almost forgotten the random VHS I'd found on the sidewalk. It wasn't so much that the unmarked tape was left on the ground, but that I'd sworn it was a home video with a woman who said my name. Of course, my brain automatically directed everything back to my name and my identity.

Bart's mouth popped open in an "O." White hairs dropped

over his forehead like antennae pointing at the ground. He stared at the VCR and then shrugged again. "I'll get more detail once I get him down to the lab, but it's pretty clear. This man was bitten and drank from. Maybe the vampire hit him afterward to try to throw off our scent." He was looking at me when he said that last word. Everybody knew I could smell emotions, and that this little gift—or curse—had roped me into more than one murder investigation.

"Good," I said as I hopped off the stool. "I was hoping to keep the VCR."

"Ew!" Hattie gasped. "It has his blood on it."

"I just meant I don't want it taken for evidence because I want the tape inside." I stooped to pick it up when Sett's fingers wrapped around my wrist.

His hold was always gentle, but this time he firmly pulled my hand away from the VCR. I frowned up at him.

The determined set of his jaw didn't budge when I narrowed my eyes. "I just want the tape."

He shook his head. "You know its evidence."

"But Bart just said—"

"I'll get it to you as soon as I can, Noema, I promise."

"But the tape won't have blood on it. All I have to do is eject it. I think it's a home video someone recorded and sent to me. They even said my name. I think. It could even be connected." The cloaked figure flashed in my mind again.

"So you're saying it's evidence."

I growled. "I'm saying it's important. Can we at least take it out and watch it together?"

He glanced at Crow. "Together?" A smirk ghosted over his mouth when he looked back at me. I'd never seen this side of Sett before. Of course, I'd been avoiding him for months now. Maybe he liked that this investigation brought us together, but the cockiness, the way he toyed with Crow...this was new.

And it made my stupid heart stutter.

All these new changes were going to be the death of me, if the tension between Crow and Sett didn't cause my heart attack first.

"Yes, together, like at the police station," I said, waving my free hand wildly.

He nodded. "After I help Bart load the body and clean up the crime scene."

As always, Sett stuck to his promise. In under two hours, we were crowded around Sett's desk at the Bewitcher's Beach Police Department, staring at the VCR. I'd already spewed everything I'd experienced with the vampire bat, the strange figure in the dark, and, well, the videotape—something of which I knew very little.

Now it was time to get the tape out.

Tight gloves barely fit over Sett's huge hands, but he pulled them on and carefully removed the VCR from a clear bag. After plugging it in, he pressed the eject button. Whirring was followed by a click when the little rectangular door popped open, but the tape didn't come out.

He tried it again. The same noises indicated the VCR was attempting to eject the tape. Nothing came out.

"It's stuck," I said.

Sett grumbled something and tried it a third time. Again, the eject button didn't eject anything.

Crow reached across the desk for the box of gloves. "Let me try. I'm good with electronics."

Sett frowned and didn't take his narrowed eyes off Crow the entire time Crow fiddled with the VCR.

A rainbow of smells wafted from Crow as he worked to get the tape. Sandalwood's confidence melted away to the pineapple pizza scent of confusion, and then finally ended with smoky frustration.

He dropped the VCR back on the desk and blew out a breath. "I can just pull it out, but it might ruin the tape."

"No!" I barked.

"Or," he continued, "I can unscrew the cover and remove the tape manually."

"That one."

Sett produced a screwdriver from one of the many drawers in his desk. It took too long for him to let go of it when Crow tugged it from Sett's fist. Crow shot him a look before unscrewing the first of four screws. The edge popped up, but when he unscrewed the others, they didn't pop up.

"It's so bent out of shape," he said. "And I think there's blood making the screws stick."

Finally, and with a little tugging, he pulled the cover off. Even the inside of the VCR was bent and damaged. He tried to tug the tape from the deck, but it was still stuck. He huffed and offered me a glancing frown. "I don't know if it's coming out undamaged."

"What if it's evidence?" I said

Sett huffed. "Now she admits it."

"Excuse me?"

"Look." The sheriff leaned both elbows on the desk, his gray eyes pinning me in the seat across from him. His heavy weight tipped the massive desk toward him. "I'm already violating policy by letting you tamper with evidence."

"Because Bart said it's not the murder weapon," I said.

"Because you're you."

Despite Crow shuffling closer to me, Sett's eyes stayed fixed on mine. Now Sett was sending me a message, and I heard it loud and clear.

I'm breaking the rules for you. Sett Lawrence, the man who never ever in one million years wanted to step outside the lines of policy, was doing it for me, and after I'd avoided him for months.

After he'd bailed me out of jail.

After we'd almost kissed.

I brushed my fang over my bottom lip again, and his eyes dipped to my mouth. Dangit. That wasn't my intention, but his gaze lingered. Maybe this was what happened when you hadn't been around the one person you couldn't stop thinking about for months. Your mind jumps right back to the last moments you spent together as if those moments were yesterday.

Of course, I hadn't seen Crow for months either. Less even, since I saw Sett around town.

Crow cursed and dropped the VCR on the desk. He'd been so focused on the tape, I didn't know if he noticed the exchange between me and Sett.

"I have to take the entire VCR apart to get it out," he said.

"Do it," Sett said without breaking eye contact.

My mouth popped open.

"You're not going to like, arrest me if this ends up being the murder weapon and it's in pieces?" Crow asked.

"If I'm arresting you, it won't be for that."

"Sett!" I squeaked. I couldn't stand it anymore. He was so... bold. And taking his frustration with me out on Crow wasn't fair.

Crow dropped both of his palms on the desk and leaned over Sett. "Hey man, what's your problem with me?" My gaze ping ponged between them.

Sett peeled his eyes off of me and stared cooly at my semi-boyfriend. "I told you. You weren't there for Noema when she needed you."

"Remind me, how's that *your* problem? You need a dose of reality, Sheriff. Noema is dating me, not you."

A horrible smell suddenly filled my nose. Charred toast sloughed off of Sett as his regret became palpable.

Regret. For not dating me before I met Crow? For arresting me last year and ruining his chances?

I squirmed in my seat. He'd more than made up for that. Not that I was keeping score. I didn't even care about it anymore.

Sett had slowly started coloring outside the lines when he was around me. This wasn't the first time he didn't follow policy for my sake.

The chair squeaked as Sett pushed it back from the desk. He stood, towering over us and forcing Crow to straighten.

Folding his arms, Sett spoke with a level voice despite the regret clouding around him. "I don't have to be dating her to care about her." Crow opened his mouth, but Sett cut him off. "It's late. I'm going to check in with Bart, so you have to leave the station. You may come back tomorrow and work on getting the tape out, but the VCR does not leave this desk."

"Can I help?" I blurted.

Sett's eyes shifted to me. "Since recent events do seem to involve you, you may officially work as my consultant."

"Isn't that a conflict of interest?" Crow asked.

We both threw him daggered glares. After a second, Sett released a joyless laugh. "I've recently come to the under-standing that life will pass you by if you don't take the opportu-nities that are presented to you." I blinked at him. My sleepy, late-night brain tried to piece together what his words meant. I'd kill for a Diet Pepsi to wake me up right now. "Conflict of interest or not, sometimes the fastest way to catch a killer is with Noema's unique skill. And if she's in any kind of danger, I'm willing to move fast. Wouldn't you agree?"

A mixture of body odor and smoke curled in my nose. Even though Crow was the one I was dating, he was both jealous of and irritated with Sett. It'd been months since we spent time together, but he should have remembered he couldn't hide his emotions from my nose.

"Agreed," he finally said.

"Good." Sett lifted his chin toward the door. "I'll see you both here tomorrow morning at nine. That is, if you want to help."

I opened my mouth but had nothing to say. I truly was speechless, and the detective didn't miss it.

Sett smiled at me and tapped his finger to his lips.

Before Crow realized what was happening, I grabbed his arm and tugged him. He spun around, and I hooked my arm through his.

It was finally time to get that Diet Pepsi and go to bed. At this point, the caffeine would just put me to sleep.

CHAPTER 6
TWO MANY BOYFRIENDS

THE NEXT MORNING, it was my turn for the summer camp dropoff—a task that'd soon be replaced by school carpools and prepping for the fall festival. Though I didn't know how many more people could fit into the tiny town for the annual autumnal celebration. The cobblestone streets were already teeming with visitors and packed with cars. Which also meant traffic would be atrocious and we needed to leave earlier and earlier for camp each day.

Getting four of my own children into the van in time was akin to running a circus with feral monkeys, but getting them ready and making it to their friends' houses on time actually helped. As it turned out, feral monkeys were motivated to get moving when their friends were on the other side of the circus.

Once we were piled inside with their friends, all seven children chattered away happily until Dio took over the conversation. One moment, Stevie and her friends were discussing the camp's craft projects, and the next, they were yelling at Dio to stop reminding them about the sports portion of the camp.

I glanced in the rearview mirror, spotting Dio's messy hair. "Not everybody wants to talk about soccer, Bud."

He slumped. "It's not even just soccer. It's every sport!"

"It *was* every sport," Jovi joined in. My studious, quiet boy didn't care for sports, but he was as naturally talented at just about any of them as Dio. "Until Mr. Pipes broke his back."

"Mr. Pipes was my faaaaavorite!" Stevie whined. "He let me collect pillbugs during baseball practice."

Of course. Any teacher who let Stevie focus on animals and insects would be her favorite teacher.

"Getting a little exercise won't hurt you, Steves," I said, glancing in the mirror again at my pouting daughter.

I eased the van into the drop off line at the edge of the elementary school. Loads of children piled out of the trail of minivans, station wagons, and my not-so-mini van. At least the Chevy Astro could fit eight of us, which made driving this horrible boxy beast worth it.

"I'll run with the forest rabbits!" she said "That can be my exercise."

Halen slid open the van door and jumped out with a cursory goodbye. Dio, Jovi, and the kids' three friends followed while Stevie hung back.

She folded her arms and pushed out her bottom lip. "Do I have to do sports? The new gym teacher is a meanie."

I twisted around in the driver's seat. "Because he won't let you play with bugs?"

"Because he doesn't like me."

I glanced at the clock. In twenty minutes, I was supposed to meet Sett at the station to listen to Olivia's alibi. If she had one. And before the meeting, I wanted to stop by Roller Shakes and ask the most fashionable vampire I knew if she'd seen another vampire around town in a shiny cloak. Cordelia's night shift usually ended before the sun came up, but with this summer being so cloudy and Crow gone more than he was running the roller rink, she'd picked up more waitressing shifts at the rink's diner. Maybe she'd even served a bottle of YumBlood to a new vampire in town.

As much as I wanted answers about the murderous vampire, Stevie's feelings were more important.

"Why do you say that?" I asked.

"Because Mr. Dylan said I'll never go to Shadowvale when I grow up if I can't focus."

He wasn't entirely wrong. Though the witch college required just as much studying as any other university, Stevie's affinity for animal communication would be praised by the professors at Shadowvale.

"It sounds like he's just saying that to push you to pay attention."

"It's mean. And it's not like he's even good at teaching. When I had to be the batter, all he said was to give the ball one hard swing over and over like that would magically make me hit the ball and make the other kids stop picking on me for missing it. He shouldn't even be a teacher."

She wasn't wrong either. If he was more attuned to his students, he'd know Stevie only responded to positive reinforcements, not threats.

"Well, Steves." I reached into the back seat and took her hand in mine, praying that the line of cars behind me would just go around.

"He said he didn't even go to Shadowvale," she said before I could continue. "So how would he know?"

"That's a good point. If you want to skip the gym portion of camp, I'll pick you up early, but you'll miss the last reading hour."

She shrugged. "It's okay. Mr. Dylan is actually really bad at pretty much all the sports we play except baseball, and it's so super funny. Yesterday, Dio had to teach him how to dribble a basketball." Giggling, she slipped her hand from mine and jumped out of the open door. "Bye Mommy!"

Just like that, she ended the whining and disappeared in the sea of summer camp kids. I shook my head and turned back to the steering wheel, whispering to myself not to speed. Sett would have a cow if I broke the law to make it to a meeting with him. Thankfully, the drive was only five minutes to Roller Shakes, which gave me two minutes to chat with Cordelia and one minute to run next door to the station.

Exactly seven minutes later, I sat across from the pinch-faced, pissed-off president of the historical society with a Diet Pepsi in hand.

I'd even brought a drink for her from Roller Shakes. Olivia nearly crushed the paper cup in her fist. Pretty soon, lemonade would spill all over the cushioned chair.

Sett had moved his desk chair and the two guest chairs to the front of the station. The main room was spacious, housing his desk, filing cabinets, an evidence closet, and a small mini kitchen. Behind his desk, a narrow hallway led to a tiny interrogation room and a single jail cell.

Instead of using the interrogation room, he posted up in the front of the main room, where he kept an eye on Crow stooping over the VCR at his desk.

"There's nothing to be angry about," Sett said to Olivia. "We're just having a conversation."

"And we had to stop construction," I added. That should make Olivia happy. Maybe it'd even stop her from smashing the cup of lemonade.

"Right," Sett said. "Until the investigation is complete, Hattie and Noema have halted the renovation."

"And what does any of this have to do with me?" she asked, her teeth clearly flat and entirely un-fanglike. But she could have filed them down after killing Ryan, right? Even if she wasn't a vampire, she could have helped in the attack. Sett wanted to clear her as a suspect first.

"One could argue that you threatened Ryan."

She bubbled her lips and released a raspberry sound. "This has to be a joke."

"I never joke about murder."

The deep tone of Sett's voice stirred something within me. My cheeks heated, and I kept my gaze pinned on Olivia so that it didn't wander to the man sitting next to me again. These feelings were inappropriate with Crow standing right behind us, but I could at least control my staring.

"Where were you around ten-thirty last night, Miss Woodstone?" Sett asked.

"I was—well." Her knuckles went white around the cup, finally crushing it once and for all. Nothing spilled out. Apparently, she'd downed all the lemonade already.

Sett leaned forward in his seat. Placing his elbows on his knees, he clasped his hands and leveled with her. "Miss Woodstone, I apologize for upsetting you, but I need you to answer the question. I truly don't mean to pry into your life. This is for the sake of a man who unjustly lost his life."

As bold as Sett had become, he was still the same man I knew before. Warm, safe, committed to both solving the crime and offering comfort to those involved.

Olivia's gaze fell to her lap where she suddenly became too interested in the empty cup. "I was at home."

I almost gagged at the sudden rush of rotten fish stench filling the air. Sett knew me well enough to know that I didn't even have to shake my head. Olivia was lying her blue pantsuit right off.

"Olivia." His voice was steady, soft even. "I'm going to need you to tell me the truth."

She smashed the cup between her palm and her leg and

relented. "Fine! I was at a town council meeting in Carmel, arguing for that ratty old Victorian cottage to be torn down." Her chest heaved as she took several quick breaths. At this rate, she'd hyperventilate.

"Miss, I'm going to get you some water, okay?" Sett stood and walked to the little kitchen, returning a moment later with a paper cup half the size of the empty one in her lap.

With shaking hands, she accepted it. She downed the water in one gulp and smashed the cup beside the other one. Her leg was quickly becoming a graveyard of paper cups. "The cottage is lowering my home's value, and I want to sell. You cannot tell the ladies at the historical society that I was there."

"How late did the meeting go?"

"Until midnight," she said. "I was there until the last vote was cast. You can ask Tammy or Drake."

She may have smelled a little nervous, but all hints of guilt had vanished. I gave Sett a quick nod before he turned back to Olivia.

"Thank you, Miss Woodstone."

When she left, Sett reached out and patted my arm. His silent appreciation warmed me. I glanced at Crow, but he was bent over the VCR, carefully taking each piece apart.

The prophecy says that every witch in the Titan family is fated to marry a reaper. As one of those witches, I shouldn't even be entertaining the feelings rising up within me whenever Sett offered me a smile or touched me. My fate was already sealed to Crow, and he was a good man, if not a little absent. But I'd become used to living with just me, my kids, and our little pet mouse. Maybe my semi-solitary life was the perfect setup to be with a man like Crow.

"Well," Sett said, "it would take way too much sunscreen for a vampire to work outside all day, so I know none of the construction crew are vampires, but I still want to speak with them about Ryan's behavior. You know, see if they noticed anyone following him lately or if he was acting unusual or frightened. You're welcome to stay if you want, but I don't think I need any help sniffing for lies."

I nodded. "That's perfect, because I've been wanting to check in with Chanel after I talked to Cordelia today." I tapped the paper cup still in my hand. Still perfectly intact, which was more than I could say for Olivia's cups. "I asked her if she would ever be caught undead wearing a cloak. She said only if it was one of Chanel's designs. Then I remembered, Chanel sells a maroon and black cloak. She might know who bought it."

Sett straightened. "That's my girl." A little gasp escaped me. I certainly wasn't *his girl*, but hearing him say it did strange things to my stomach. "I knew you'd speed up this investigation."

I gritted my teeth before a giggle popped out of me. Here I was acting like a schoolgirl with a crush again, and right in front of the guy I was fated to marry.

"Check back in with me after you talk to Chanel."

I swallowed a sudden smile, because why couldn't I wait to do exactly that? I jumped out of my seat and squeaked a general goodbye to both Sett and Crow. They responded at the exact same time and then shot each other a glare.

I ducked out the front door before the tension snapped. I needed to get away from them and soak in the fresh air. The walk to Chanel's would do me good.

FALL WAS JUST around the corner, and I could already smell the campfire smoke mixed in with the briny breeze and pine. I drew a long breath just before I stepped into Chanel's boutique.

Heady jasmine perfume assaulted me, and I nearly stumbled back out over the threshold, but spotting Chanel's platinum blonde hair across the racks of dresses had me pressing forward. A man—another man—died at Mockbuster, and Sett had asked me to assist with the investigation this time. I had a duty to brave the nauseating perfume. Justice for Ryan. Not to mention his girlfriend deserved answers. I knew how the medical accident had ended my late husband's life; I couldn't imagine not knowing.

Bright orange and violet dresses caught my eye as I scanned the tall racks for any familiar cloaks.

"Someone's here," Chanel said. My wolf ears perked, catching the click of a phone put back on the receiver.

My gaze snapped toward her. "Hey Chanel," I said as I emerged from between the dresses and intimate lacy sleepwear. "It's just me."

Her face was bare of makeup, dewy and shimmering with natural beauty, but the heavy look tugging at the corners of her eyes had nothing to do with her lack of makeup. Her hair was pulled back in a hurried bun with tendrils escaping every which way. Chanel could pull off the messy look effortlessly, but it was still a shock to see her like this. Never had I witnessed her so visibly....off.

She smoothed her palm over one side of her head and cleared her throat. Straightening from behind the glass countertop, she tapped long pink nails against it. A nervous reaction? Or did she just like the sound of the tap, tap, tap?

"Noema," she said. "What can I help you with?"

That was it? Chanel spoke smoothly, always with a compliment, a quip, or a subtle piece of advice about dressing nicer.

"Is everything okay?" I glanced toward the landline phone next to her cash register. "I didn't mean to interrupt."

"No interruption." She shrugged, suddenly too interested in wiping imaginary dust off the glass counter.

A whiff of her pungent nerves mingled with the cloud of jasmine. Anxiety? From Chanel? I had to have been imagining this. Nothing threw this woman off her perfectly balanced stilettos.

She sniffed and gave me a stiff smile. "One of these days, I'm going to get you into an evening gown."

I smirked. This was the Chanel I knew. She always threatened to do a makeover on me like I was an awkward teenage girl in a rom-com who only needed to remove her glasses to win her first kiss. I needed less men in my life, not more.

"And where in Bewitcher's Beach would I wear an evening gown?"

"The bar at The Oyster Inn is fancy when Barney works his fairy magic," she said. "You could wear it on a date with Crow." Her eyes sparkled, and one corner of her plump lips curved. "Or Sett."

My tongue seemed to swell, and my throat caught a cough. I palmed my chest at the same time I shook my head. "What?"

"Or both," she teased. "I'm not judging a girl who likes to keep her options open."

"No that's—"

"Girl." She leaned forward, dainty elbows balanced against the glass. Her thick lashes curled into her eyebrows as she looked up at me. "I don't blame you. Crow's the bad boy, but Sett, he's basically your family. If I didn't know you two better, I'd think you were the sheriff's wife."

"Why would you say that?"

Her devilish grin flattened for a moment before it stretched again. A strange mixture of smells wafted from her. Ammonia, then sandalwood, then fish. Fear, confidence, guilt, followed by a hint of regret's burnt toast, then back to confidence.

She lifted one delicate shoulder in another shrug. Jutting her chin toward the phone, her doe eyes looked me up and down. "I've only got one boyfriend, but you're making two look fun."

"Chanel!"

A little laugh escaped her. "Sorry, Noema. I really don't mean to upset you, I think I'm just willing to say what nobody else will. You're prophesied to marry a reaper, right? But Sett, well, everybody can see you two fit more perfectly than my curves in a cocktail dress."

I cleared my throat. My stupid tongue didn't seem to fit where it belonged. Lifting my chin, I forced a neutral look on my face and changed the subject. "I'm glad to hear you're dating again." Chanel's previous boyfriend had been decades older than her. He passed peacefully from old age several months back. "But I didn't realize you had a boyfriend. I thought you wanted to go on a date with Ryan before he..." My voice faded.

She popped up from her casual position leaning on the countertop and busied herself by tapping buttons on the register. "Yes, well, I learned from the best." She slid her eyes to me, pinning me with a precarious look. "Keeping my options open, and all that."

I narrowed my eyes, but it was hard to stay mad at Chanel for too long. When people spoke the truth, as she often and bluntly did, I appreciated it. That was almost the entire basis of my friendship with Hattie. In a world full of people who lie, and with every lie stinking like rotten fish, I never held a grudge against a truthsayer.

"So." I turned the mischievous glint back on her with wide eyes. "Do I know him?"

"Who?" She didn't take her eyes off the screen as she tapped away on the keyboard.

"Your boyfriend."

Finally, her gaze shifted back to me. Her tongue flicked out over her lips. "I'm...not sure."

I almost gagged when the lie hit me like a dead fish to the face. And yes, I'd had that happen once when I went for a run at the beach on two legs. Never again. I'd always run in my wolf form so that I didn't trip and fall in the sand.

Chanel lied? *Chanel*? And about this? She obviously didn't want me to know her boyfriend, and I couldn't blame her. My personal affairs were too public. Almost everybody's affairs were too known by all of Bewitcher's Beach. If I could take back sharing the prophecy and my complaints about Crow's traveling, I would. The whole town didn't need to know my conundrum.

I sucked in a breath. No point in pushing her when it wasn't my business. Besides, she'd already moved on, busying herself with a new design. She pulled fabric onto the desk and plucked at crooked threads with a seamripper. When the stitches were too stubborn, she pulled out a small pair of scissors and snipped the thread.

The fabric reminded me what I'd really come here for. "Anyway, I was wondering if you knew who you sold a certain cloak to." Describing the cloak, she lit up enough to lose interest in her project.

Chanel dropped the seam ripper and smoothed out the fabric in front of her as she spoke. "Oh that garment was beautiful. Heavy fabric so it would drape over the shoulders rather than laying stiffly." She gestured to her own shoulders. "Sewn with these brand new enchanted threads so that its existence suspends when its wearer shifts forms. The same magic I told you I could put into an evening gown for you. You could drop into your furry form and it'd simply wait in the ether until you became human again. No losing clothes."

I had to admit, that sounded convenient, but Chanel's clothing wasn't exactly my style and was lightyears beyond my budget. Though the bat and the dark figure in the night came to mind.

"So you know who bought it?"

"I never forget a piece of fashion, but I can't say who purchased it." I took a small sniff. No fish. "Tourists are the majority of my business, and I don't exactly commit their faces to memory. Let me pull up a record to see if they paid with a check." After a moment, her flat mouth dipped. "Cash. Let's see when they bought it—Oh!" Her brows peaked. "This last weekend. Friday night."

The night before I was attacked by the bat. The night before I saw the figure in this cloak staring at me from across town.

They'd bought the cloak to shift into a bat and then back into a vampire...

"Yes," she continued, unaware of how thick my tongue felt in my throat and that I wouldn't be able to respond until I cleared my head. "I remember it was a busy night. Rush of customers. I'm sorry I can't give you more details. Is this about the investigation?" Her voice pitched higher. Or was that my imagination?

I coughed and reflected the shrugs she'd given me back at her. "I'm not sure."

The bat, the figure, the dead man. They had to be pieces of the same puzzle, and now that I had this extra thread tying them together, an enchanted thread, it was time Sett saw the connection too.

CHAPTER 7
THE END

BY THE TIME Sett recorded the information I shared, Crow was done for the night, declaring that he needed more time to get the VHS out without destroying it.

Without the video to distract me, I wanted to throw myself at tracking clues, but we had very little to go on and the day was already slipping into twilight. Plus, I'd promised Crow a date before he had to pop over to the next town for a quick job with his Calling. Though I didn't know if sharing a strawberry milkshake at Roller Shakes counted as a date at our age.

We'd sat staring at one another before he hopped up to retrieve our milkshake, leaving me surrounded by swarming young couples that seemed more in love than us.

Rock beats boomed from Roller Shakes' sound system. Teenagers skated over the psychedelic carpet and onto the wooden rink where they held hands and laughed. Thankfully, word of the murder hadn't spread across Bewitcher's Beach just yet. People still enjoyed the feeling of safety that we'd been soaking up for the past few months.

And maybe it wasn't just a feeling at all. Ryan was attacked by a vampire, and I was attacked by a bat, but the violence was only around us. No other attacks were reported, which meant this could simply be a rogue vampire who'd already passed through town.

The question was, why focus on me and Ryan? Why return to Mockbuster?

The questions slipped away as Crow approached the booth. A pink milkshake topped with foamy whipped cream looked out of place in his hand. He set it on the vinyl table between us and offered me a tired smile.

As I stared at the two crossing straws like a treasure map's X over our dessert drink, Chanel's words needled me.

If I didn't know you better, I'd think you were the sheriff's wife. Ugh. That didn't sit right with me while I was dating someone else—the person I suspected was mentioned in my family's prophecy.

Crow knew about the prophecy as well as anyone, but he'd brushed it off when I told him. As was expected for a guy who took matters into his own hands, naturally shirking constraints like trends and rules and, well, prophecies. He didn't even believe in it.

Nothing outside of his Calling could force Crow into anything he didn't want to do. Not even a fated future. So when I'd told him about it, he chalked it up to a shrug and reminded me to choose whatever I wanted in my life.

The problem was, I didn't know what I wanted.

I eyed Crow from across the table. Neon blue and purple lights shone through his thick curls. He brushed an overgrown lock of hair out of his face as he pulled the straw toward him. His chin and cheekbones were all cutting angles, fiercely handsome like a model in a magazine. Someone far away that I didn't truly know.

Crow caught my gaze and gave me a smirk. Taking a sip of the milkshake, his lips quickly flipped.

"I know you can't have chocolate, but I don't know if I can stomach strawberry," he said after several minutes of silence. We didn't have as much to talk about after months apart as I'd expected. He'd already shared with me the highlights of his Calling trip, and I told him about the time Stevie got stuck in a tree trying to talk to a squirrel who'd lost his magic. The longer the story had gone on, the less eager Crow's nods became. I'd cut the story short when the minty smell of his curiosity completely vanished.

He tried another sip of the shake and then shook his head. "This is truly terrible. I'm really a chocolate kind of guy."

"Until your menu includes a Diet Pepsi milkshake, strawberry is the superior flavor," I teased.

He didn't take the bait. Instead, he plucked his straw from the glass and set it on a napkin before pushing the milkshake across the table. "Maybe next time we should get two different milkshakes?"

I nodded and tried to smile when a rush of icy air startled me. We both flicked our attention to an incoming ghost. In a blur of gold, Hattie zipped from the front entrance to the cafe, weaving between teenagers and tables. The fringe of her dress shimmered with the bright colors of Roller Shakes's wild designs. A look of panic pinched her brows beneath her headband.

"He's coming," she shrieked as she hovered over us, her transparent body slipping into the solid table.

My hackles instantly raised as possibilities hurtled through my mind. "Who?"

"Our patron." Her voice was deadpanned, which was actually very unusual for Hattie, even though she was technically dead. I leaned forward, mouth popping open. "That was my face too when he called. Rufus Harrington is coming to Everland Theater to ensure that the project continues despite this little...upset. And, let's just say, he's also upset. With us."

My mouth hung open as my brain went paralytic. Of course he was upset; it made perfect sense. He'd dumped a lot of money into this theater's transformation, specifically, so that he could play his supernatural-focused films here and draw the niche crowd of magical people into the world of Hollywood. These were people who'd formerly shown little interest in movies, and I couldn't blame them since none of the stories represented our lives as supernaturals.

Now the project had lost its head of construction—the owner of the specific construction company that Rufus had insisted we hired.

Finally, my mind connected with my tongue. "What does he expect us to do when this is out of our control?"

Hattie shook her head. "Big wigs like him don't care about the details, they just want it done, and we've already lost two days toward the deadline."

I blew out a breath. "Okay, it's all okay. We can figure this out." Did I believe that? "We just need to come up with a plan to present to him when he arrives."

She folded her arms and swayed side to side, too antsy to stand still. "Now we're talking. We need to get this show on the road because he's already in Bewitcher's Beach, on a little getaway with his wife. But we won't see him at Everland Theater until tomorrow morning because he promised his wife a night at the beach."

I nearly swallowed my tongue. Running my fingers through my hair, I stole a look at Crow. "I'm sorry," I said when he met my gaze. "I'm going to have to skip out on our date early and figure this out."

"Nonsense!" Hattie stared down at him. "Crow loves a bit of drama as much as me. Isn't that right?"

I snorted. "He did not sign up for a brainstorming session when he agreed to this date. He can listen in while we panic, though. If a werewolf and a ghost having a joint emotional breakdown isn't absolute cinema, I don't know what is."

Crow folded his arms. "How about Crow speaks for himself?" His eyes shifted between us, and that smirk hovered mischievously. "You're both right. I can help and be amused at the same time. And would you look at this? I'm here for you when Sett isn't." He leaned back into the booth, getting comfortable in his competitiveness. Something about his claim didn't feel as helpful as he likely intended for it to sound.

This morning's questioning session with Olivia was not an interrogation, and bragging to Sett didn't sit right with me. Also, he hadn't dragged me anywhere. I wanted to investigate, and Crow knew that as well as anyone.

I frowned. This comparison gave me the same icky feeling as the night Crow found me with the bat bites. Sett did what needed to be done while Crow...well, he'd complained about Sett helping. To no fault of his own, though. Crow had a right to be annoyed when Sett overstepped, same as I would be if another woman did that with him.

But I didn't have a right to *enjoy it* when Sett overstepped. Not while dating another man.

Crow scooted in, and Hattie dropped into the seat beside him, hovering more than sitting. "So," she started, "Rufus wanted this project headed by Ryan. But Ryan is dead. No ghost. But, *but*, we finalized all the plans with Ryan before he was..." Her eyes scanned the rink, likely to see if any children were nearby before speaking the M word aloud. Though Roller Shakes was open twenty-four hours, young kids didn't frequent it at night. The evenings were for teenagers' dates. "Murdered," she continued. "So I think if we show Rufus everything we'd set out to do, I can head the projects. I'm used to running full casts of up to sixty people. Surely directing a construction project can't be harder than running a live theater show. It's all about communication. The only issue is the construction crew won't listen to me."

I frowned. "How do you know they won't listen to you? Have you tried talking with them?"

"Yes. They can't do anything without a manager's approval."

"There it is!" I clapped my hands. "All we have to do is be the go-betweens from the crew to the owner of the company."

"Or have them place a new manager in Ryan's spot?" Crow suggested.

"No can do," I said. "The company is small. Ryan was the only manager. This is the only crew."

Hattie wiped her palm over her forehead. "I would say I'm embarrassed that I didn't think of simply getting the owner's approval, but I don't really get embarrassed."

Crow laughed again. When was the last time I made him laugh? I worried him. I complained about him. I liked him and how adventurous he was, but I didn't need him to encourage me to take risks or be spontaneous. I could do that just fine all on my own.

"Then it's solved," he said. "Just tell Rufus Hattie will be communicating everything to the owner to keep the project on track."

She nodded and blew out a breath that I guessed would smell of relief if I could scent a ghost's emotions.

"Panic mode off," I said, giving her a reassuring grin.

Hattie popped back to her feet. "That was short and sweet. I'll let you two finish your date."

Before we could respond, she surged away, taking the blast of cold air with her.

We were left in silence, eyeing each other with nothing

particularly interesting to say. All of the excitement had come and left with Hattie. It was a whirlwind that I strangely missed. The distraction had swept Chanel's words away.

Now they returned, louder.

Two boyfriends.

Crow hadn't signed up for *that* either. Chanel had said Sett and I fit together even though we were opposites. He drove me crazy with his rules and regulations. Sett frustrated me like... like someone you know inside and out. Like a best friend, a family member—like my late husband did when he insisted I make a promise to finish writing a screenplay.

The silence stagnated. The only sounds came from the rink's speakers blasting "How Do I Live" by LeAnn Rimes, the roll of wheels over the wooden floor, and teenagers giggling.

We didn't come close to giggling.

Crow forced a strained smile. "You can finish this if you want." He nudged the milkshake glass closer to me, but my stomach suddenly turned. Bitterness stained my tongue. I'd been avoiding Sett for months now, but it wasn't what I truly wanted. My giggles were proof of it. Chanel knew it, and deep down, I knew it too.

Even if Crow didn't believe in the prophecy, I did. I carried the thought around with me that I was bound to him because of who the other women in my family had married. But he was right. I could make my own decisions, and I decided this date— and this milkshake—wasn't fair for me to enjoy. Not with how much Crow hated the strawberry flavor, and not when Sett kept popping up in my head.

And apparently, popping up in Crow's head too. Crow was competitive, but it seemed to have more to do with proving himself than me. Why else would he want Sett to know about how he was here for me during tonight's mini crisis?

I sucked in a breath. "Crow." He met my gaze, and for a

moment, I thought he could read my mind or smell my emotions. I definitely stank of a mixture of rain, pineapple pizza, and burnt toast. Burnt pizza rain? After years of mostly ignoring my emotion's scents, sadness, confusion, and regret laced my breath, and I didn't try to bury them this time. It was okay to hurt a little with what I was about to do.

"You want to end the date early?" he guessed.

"I want to end..." My wolf ears folded back. "Us."

To my surprise, the ghost of relief flashed across his face. My brow furrowed, and he leaned forward, reaching across the table to take my hand in his. "I like you Noema. You're fierce and determined and a little wild." My wolf fever burned even hotter over my cheeks and throat. "But I don't think I can be here the way you need me to be."

I nodded. "You need a woman who likes the space your lifestyle will give her." Like Chanel and her out-of-town boyfriend.

"And I just can't keep up with Sett," he said. "And frankly, I don't want to have to keep trying."

"It's not a competition."

He released my hand. "Not anymore. I like to win, but you're not a game. You deserve better."

Me? No, he was the one who deserved to date someone who only had eyes for him. I'd been selfish and stupid to force this relationship to continue all for the sake of a prophecy tied to a family I didn't even know. Maybe I wanted it to be true, because if my life followed the prophecy, it'd connect me across time and space to the mother and father, the grandparents, and the relatives I never got to love.

Maybe if marrying a reaper was truly my fate, I wouldn't have to force it.

"I'm sorry," I whispered. "We had fun."

"We did. And I know we still will. We're friends." He stood

and grinned down at me. "Make sure you invite me to the next emotional breakdown by my favorite werewolf and ghost. Got it?"

Before I could respond, the air pressure in Roller Shakes suddenly shifted. The entrance door slammed shut just as the song faded into silence. Was it colder in here? Nobody else seemed to notice. Not even Crow turned to see who'd just stepped inside, but something about the man and woman marching into the cafe was oddly familiar. Like they were celebrities I'd only seen on TV.

I blinked as they came closer, and I spotted the man's wispy nutmeg combover and faintly purple eyes. With the smile stretching his face, I almost didn't recognize him.

"Noema?" Crow said.

I nodded half-heartedly and mumbled, "Got it."

Inviting him to our next breakdown would be easy enough because it would be tomorrow morning when we had a meeting with Rufus Harrington—the man who'd just stepped inside Roller Shakes. The man I only recognized from pictures in the newspaper when his first film went big. The man who never smiled in said pictures because he had...fangs.

Our patron was a vampire.

CHAPTER 8
VAMPIRE HOUR

SLEEP CAME in fits and starts. If I wasn't tossing, I was turning theories over in my head. Why would the person who poured money into Everland Theater's transformation want to kill the man in charge of said transformation?

"Because he doesn't want to pay for it anymore." A deadpan voice ripped me from my state of semi-consciousness.

Someone was inside my room.

I shot forward in bed, my heart hammering as hard as if I'd just finished a run along the beach. After the bat's intrusions, my defenses were on the edge of a cliff, and I couldn't hold back from shifting. My fingers grew into claws and fur sprouted across my body. My nightgown slipped off of me and mixed with the tangled sheets and bedquilt. Before I knew it, I had transformed into my wolf self.

My tail was lifted, ears perked, black lips curled back to bare my canines. Fur was raised in a line down my back as full-defense mode triggered. Whoever was in my house, where my babies slept, was about to get a full set of wolf teeth sunk into them.

In the dim light, I had no problem spotting the ghost

haunting my room. I released a growl of frustration, and the spiked fur slowly settled.

Hattie shook her head at me, clearly disappointed by my reaction. "You'd think by now you'd be used to me haunting your house."

Not after the bat's attack, and really, I'd never been exactly fond of this jump-scare tactic for waking me up. But Hattie did what Hattie wanted and trying to reason with a one-hundred-and-four-year-old ghost—if you counted her living years too—was fruitless. I still barked at her anyway to let her know I didn't appreciate being startled. This was simply one of Hattie's personality quirks that you had to accept if you wanted to be her friend.

Her eyes rolled so far back into her head that I could have mistaken her for a poltergeist. She waved a wispy hand. "Your sleep talking has gotten worse. Anyway, once you're not naked, meet me downstairs."

I tilted my head and whined.

"We have to talk about Rufus. I mean, you were doing a fabulous job talking about him in your sleep. And yes, I have my own theories now that we know he's a vampire, so we need to discuss this before a potential murderer marches into Everland Theater."

To prod her, I whined again and released a bubbling bark.

"I don't think he wants to be our patron anymore," she said as a reminder.

I danced nervously on my front paws, my legs tangling in the sheets and nightgown. Tossing my snout back, I growled again.

"If you want the juicy details, shift back and get your clothes on." She floated away, pausing halfway inside the wood of the closed bedroom door. "I'll tell you what I found out when you meet me downstairs."

Once she vanished, I mustered every bit of energy I could to change myself back into my human body. Normally, it'd take time and rest to reset before I could transform again, but the fitful night of sleep gave me a small well of energy to pull from that I hadn't used yet today.

Back on two feet, I nearly buckled at the knees. I slid off the bed, my legs now liquid and shaking from the effort of shifting back and forth. The clock on my bedside table blared green numbers that told me it was far too early in the day to be this tired. I was usually still snoring at five thirty in the morning.

An ice cold Diet Pepsi would help. Maybe three.

I tugged on a pair of jeans and a wrinkled Shadowvale University sweatshirt. Pausing at the floor length mirror pinned up behind my door, I snorted at the reflection of bedhead and bare feet. Chanel was going to have a hell of a time getting me into an evening gown. Not because I didn't want to dress up, but because this was the usual garb of a busy mom of four. Dressing fancy when you spent half your life between a sticky mini van and an even stickier video rental shop was absurd.

Yawning, I trudged into the kitchen on autopilot and set out four Darkwing Duck bowls with plastic spoons balanced on the edge of each one. In the center of the table, I lined up four boxes of cereal, one for each child's preference, and then grabbed two bottles of Diet Pepsi from the fridge.

I gulped half of one on my way down to the shop, where I spotted Hattie pacing the length of the aisle full of horror movies. Fitting. Her perpetual glow brightened only an arm's length around her like a moving lantern.

"So," I said as I set about my normal routine, grabbing the video return box and dragging it to the front desk. "You discovered something about Rufus?"

My stomach clenched. If only I could blame the binge of caffeine and bubbles, but just the thought of the vampire I'd spotted last night set me on edge. If that combover creep had burst into my bedroom as a bat and bit me, I wanted Sett to lock him away, immediately. But first, I had to prove Rufus was the same vampire who drained the life out of Ryan.

Hattie froze, but the fringe on her dress did not. Like nervous little worms wriggling all around her, the glittering strips of fabric swayed for a moment before falling still. Everything was turning my stomach this morning thanks to that nightmarish sleep. Dreams of vampire fangs sinking into my arm plagued me in the wee hours.

Hattie sucked in a breath, mimicking the physiological reaction of breathlessness that she'd have if her emotions were still in a living body. "Yes. Rufus's last film tanked. Actually, his last seven movies performed so badly at the box office that I hadn't even heard of them. Truthfully, I thought he was just taking time off, or working quietly on a big project."

I stopped stacking the returned VHS tapes and stared at her. "So he's lost money."

She nodded. "A lot."

"How long has he been a vampire? Maybe he wasn't concerned about money." I tried to reason the icky feeling away, hoping Rufus wasn't the bat in my bedroom. Really, anybody would have unsettled me in the same way. Simply putting a face to the bat left me tense because now it felt real, like a real murderer could have shifted into an innocent looking little creature and flown through my bedroom window. "I've heard immortality really helps in the financial department. Plus, he doesn't have to spend on healthcare."

"How would I know? I told you last night when you were practically peeing your pants after seeing him at the rink, I had no idea he was a vampire now. I had no idea a half-fae man could even become a vampire."

"Half-fae means half-human too." And humans were easy to turn into vampires, at least as far as I understood it.

"So he's half-fae, half-vampire now?"

I shook my head. Though Hattie was a ghost who lived in Bewitcher's Beach, she hadn't been alive during a time when supernaturals were well known. Some of the nuances of magical people still slipped between the cracks of her understanding. "He's all vampire now. You're either alive as whatever you are, human, half-fae, shifter, or you're undead as a vampire. All or nothing."

Hattie hummed her understanding in a haunting and shrill tone. "A vampire with a combover and money problems." Her humming turned into a whistle. "No wonder the guy turned to murder."

I stared at her over the stack of VHS tapes. "Don't remind me." Goosebumps prickled over my arms. At least I'd received the rabies shot in case Rufus was unclean, but that did nothing to soothe the icky wave of nausea rising in my throat. "We have to talk to him, in like"—I checked the clock on the yellow wall across the shop—"one hour."

"You told Sett, right?"

I shook my head. "I didn't have the frame of mind last night to do anything. Hattie...I broke up with Crow."

Her jaw dropped open, but she quickly clamped it shut again. Licking her lips, she opened her mouth. "You're saying you dumped the sexiest man to have ever set foot in Bewitcher's Beach?"

"Hattie!"

"What?" She shrugged. "This is Crow we're talking about. Curly hair, brooding face, troublemaker."

"Hattie." I tried to stop her, but she was already on a tangent. Her arms were flinging about as she raved on and on about Crow's good looks and bad boy nature. Her tangent so entirely consumed her that she paid no attention to the four werewolf kids who pounded down the steps one after another. The entire staircase shook and they all shouted their goodbyes and blew me sloppy kisses as they ran out the back door to catch the carpool.

When the tornado of children settled, I tuned back into Hattie's rant.

"Crow reaps lost spirits like me, which by all logic means that I shouldn't even like the guy if I'm happy with my existence here, and yet, I still think he's...what do the kids say these days?" When she paused for a moment, I tried to get a word in, but it was useless. "He's fiiiiine."

"You're not a lost spirit. You know exactly where you want to be, and it's here."

"Don't try to change the subject. We're talking about you and Crow. Could you imagine the look of the babies you'd have? Both of your curly manes together, and with an actress as an aunt like me, that child would be the next Shirley Temple."

"We would never have had children."

"Bah!"

"He's not a family guy."

She wiggled her eyebrows. "I know. He's the bad boy. He's every guy in every film I've ever loved."

"Hattie..."

"He's like the mobsters I used to date in Hollywood but less dangerous, which actually means he's the perfect man."

Did she seriously just call my ex-boyfriend the perfect man right in front of me? If I were still in my wolf form, I would have snapped at the air in front of her or given her a good growl. Instead, I slammed my palms against the top of the desk. The leaning tower of video tapes almost toppled, but I didn't even flinch.

I pinned her with as fierce a look as I could give her in my human form. "Hattie Marie Sharpe, you're my best friend, which means you're supposed to comfort me during a breakup, not make me feel worse."

Her hand shot to her mouth, and her face suddenly softened like a hardened statue slowly melting. "I am so very sorry." It didn't sound genuine enough to quell my irritation. I wished I could smell a ghost's emotions right about now. "I truly am, Noema. I wasn't thinking. You know how I go off."

I did, but that didn't excuse her behavior. I absentmindedly scratched at the bite marks on my arm.

"I'm broken up about it." It wasn't entirely a lie, but I still smelled the faint ick of rotten fish. My guilt welled up again, and I knew it wouldn't fade until I admitted the whole truth. She brushed her transparent fingers over my arm. The chill of her form seeped into the fabric of my sweatshirt, and I appreciated the opportunity to cool off. My werewolf fever had burned hotter ever since my mind started spinning around Rufus and vampires and video shop murders.

"You'll get over him," Hattie said. "You were never the one to go for the bad boys anyway. You're bad enough for one couple."

I sprouted a sudden laugh.

"What?" she squeaked. "You've been arrested how many times?"

Arrested, and then released by Sett the first time. Arrested and then rescued by Sett the second time. We weren't a couple —just a couple of friends—but Hattie wasn't wrong about how I needed someone a little more rule-oriented in my life to balance me out.

I blew out a breath, and my shoulders deflated. "I meant that I'm broken up about the prophecy. I gave up my reaper, so who does that make me now? I'm not a Titan woman." I referred to the family name mentioned in the prophecy.

Though I had proof that Titan was once my true surname from a newspaper article Sett had found, I hadn't yet adopted the name. In Bewitcher's Beach, I still went by Noema Wolf. I wasn't really a part of the Titans, not yet, not when I didn't even know who the Titans were and if they wanted me...

Emotion choked my throat.

"Noema." Hattie's voice was softer than I'd ever heard it. "When you came to Bewitcher's Beach, grieving over Christopher, I remember thinking that you and your children were the perfect family. Do you want to know why?" I could only shrug as I swallowed back a sudden rush of tears. "Because underneath the grief, you were all so happy. Your children were truly happy, and you all love each other so much. Why do you think I hold onto Bette so tightly?"

I lifted one shoulder and let it fall limply like a pouting child.

"Because I'm trying to force it," she said. "We haven't been close as mother and daughter since..." Her words faded, and without smelling it, I knew that if she had a body, Hattie's sadness would fill the room with the scent of fresh-fallen rain. She straightened her spine and forced out the rest of the sentence. "Since we were alive." I bit my lip. I knew exactly why they weren't close anymore, but I'd told Hattie before, and it slipped through her ears as easily as liquid flowed through her transparent body. "You don't need anyone else to make you a family. Not the other Titans, and certainly not a man."

"I know, I just thought—" I wiped a palm over my face. Exhaustion creeped in, and I reached for the second bottle of Diet Pepsi. Taking a swig, I soaked the moment of refreshment and forced the rest of the confession out. "I thought that if I fulfilled the prophecy, they'd come find me somehow. I don't know."

"That's not how fate works. You make your own."

I smirked. "You sound like Crow. He didn't believe in it either."

"That's because we're both rebels." She winked. "Prophecy or not, we break the mold, just like I did when I was an unmarried mother in 1920s Hollywood." Hattie didn't talk about her murder very often. It'd been left unsolved all these years, and she had no desire to look into it. Both she and Bette were shot during the premier for one of Hattie's films. The last thing Hattie had heard as a living, breathing woman was that she was a disgrace to women everywhere for touting her rebellious lifestyle. She was the flapper girl of all flapper girls, the one who shirked societal norms in the spotlight.

Not everybody liked that, and certainly not the man who'd held the gun that ended Hattie's life.

"Let's prepare for Rufus's arrival," she said, suddenly switching the subject.

"Right." I spun around and grabbed the phone mounted on the wall. "I'll call Sett."

But the other line trilled endlessly with no response. Sett must not have been at the station yet, so I tried his home phone. Nothing but his answering machine responded. Finally, I tried his cell phone. It was a new addition, and one that he hoped was going to replace his pager.

Though it was attached to his belt at all times, he still didn't answer, which meant he was in the middle of something. Maybe Sett already caught on to the angry vampire visiting town. Maybe we wouldn't have to have a meeting with a pissed-off-patron-slash-possible-murderer at all.

"Nothing?" Hattie asked.

I slammed the phone back on the receiver and shook my head. "Nothing."

"I'll pop over to the station and find him."

"What if Rufus gets here while you're gone?"

She shrugged. "You've dealt with murderers before." Easy for a dead woman to say; she couldn't get killed again and she didn't feel pain.

"Not murderers who have business tied up with me specifically."

Hattie's eyelids drooped to accentuate how unimpressed she was by my fear. "I might be the rebel in this friendship, but you're the bad girl." She wasn't wrong. I even owned a black leather jacket, and I technically had a criminal record. "I don't have a lick of worry for you. If Rufus is locked down anywhere other than in handcuffs, it's with you."

"You're joking."

"I only joke if it's written into the script, my darling." She gave me her signature wink, her thick eyelashes falling and rising with just the right amount of speed.

"Fine, but let me try calling the station one more time." I spun around and unhooked the phone.

"Besides," she continued. "From the back, you could pass as Ryan. You should spook Rufus out and make him think he accidentally turned the guy he tried to murder into a vampire, and that he's come back for revenge."

"I'm not an actress like you." I threw the response out over my shoulder as the phone continued ringing in my opposite ear.

The connection ended with Sett sounding robotic from the recording on the station's answering machine.

Before I turned back around, Hattie had vanished with an announcement that she'd be back in a flash. I sighed and flopped onto the stool, downing another swish from my second bottle.

Did I look that much like Ryan? Our shaggy waves were the same color, and he was short for a man while I stood tall as a woman. If my ears were tucked back under a baseball cap like the one he often wore, someone might mistake us.

Someone might have mistaken him for me.

My heart stuttered. The bat came for me, but the vampire got him. Had the killer returned for me and found Ryan in the shop alone?

I threw back another gulp of soda as if I could wash the thought away. There was no reason for anybody to kill me—that I knew of.

What had the woman in the VHS tape said?

This is a warning...

CHAPTER 9
ATTACK DOG

THE BELL chimed above Mockbuster's door, rattling loud enough to vibrate through my bones. I jumped up from the stool at the sight of a hooded man. Shadows shrouded his face, but the glint of white fangs reflected the gleam of fluorescent lights.

Sickness sloshed in my belly, or maybe it was from too much breakfast soda. Sett always said breakfast soda wasn't a thing and tried to get me to switch to fruit smoothies, but those didn't taste like crisp caffeine.

My fingernails slowly stretched into thick, sharp claws, but I clenched my fists and resisted the fight or flight response. As a human, I could talk with Rufus and reason with him. And if he decided to attack, it'd be a battle of werewolf versus vampire. I only hoped I was the faster supernatural.

With long strides, Rufus reached the front desk in only four steps. He wasn't particularly tall, not Sett height anyway, but he was taller than me. Tall enough to whack Ryan over the head easily and then bite him. Tall enough for me to have to look up at those amethyst-tinted eyes glowing beneath the hood.

My throat muscles worked through a hard swallow, and I had to dig my claws deeper into my palms to hold my form steady. It was akin to holding back a building sneeze or a sudden fit of coughs when you're in the middle of the grocery store and don't want the whole store to think you're sick.

Those purple eyes flicked to my arms, where fur slowly filled in my bare skin. His stare snapped back to my eyes. When he raised both hands, I stepped back, stumbling against the stool behind me. My canines had stretched to fangs and caught on my lower lip with sharp tips.

He merely gripped the edges of the hood and tossed it off his head. Shaking his head, he smoothed the flyaways from his combover back down to cover his bald spot.

"I didn't mean to scare you," he said, all friendly smiles but with his own fangs exposed.

I forced a grin that only ended with my fangs digging deeper into my lip. Wincing, I swallowed the growl in my throat and tried to take him at face value. He was smiling, after all. Though I'd seen murderers smile before, and if he considered me *his* breakfast drink, maybe that was reason enough for that grin.

He grabbed the front of the hood, and I suddenly zeroed in on the fine fabric, the shimmer of red. Was it the same cloak I'd seen on the figure the night of the bat's first visit? The sheen of the fabric identified it as satin, and the way it was draped elegantly over his shoulders in a perfect fit nearly confirmed my belief that this cloak was one of Chanel's designs. The cheap polyester and cotton capes we used for plays at Everland Theater looked nothing like the real thing, and for miles around, the real thing could only be purchased from Chanel.

Lifting the satin, he said, "It's for protection from the sun, of course. Didn't think I'd have to explain myself here, though. I thought Bewitcher's Beach was full of supernaturals, vampires included."

I cleared my throat. "Yeah–uh, yes. Bewitcher's Beach is a supernatural's haven, but we're a small town and with a slower pace of life, so our local vampires just sleep during the day. Nobody expects them to be out in daylight hours, so the whole cloak thing is a bit new." He nodded, and before he could speak, I continued. "I guess vampires around here are just a little more relaxed, you know? They never shift into bats either, because let's face it..." I mustered a bit of courage to lean over the front desk so that I could speak conspiratorially, like we were friends sharing a secret. "Those of us who shift into animal forms can start acting a little too much like animals when we're on all fours."

His brow pinched. "I'm not following."

"Oh you know..." I twisted my lips. "We wolves might bite if we get too hungry. Would you say it's the same for bats?"

Shaking his head, he glanced around the empty shop and then coughed. "Are you Ms. Wolf?"

I sucked in a breath. He smelled of gasoline—the impatience that often fanned into the smoky fire of anger. But it wasn't alone. A mix of pineapple pizza pinned him as confused as he was impatient.

"Ms. Titan, actually," I said, though I didn't believe it. Keeping him in the dark about my identity felt safest right now.

"Oh, I was looking for a werewolf named Noema. She's a friend of Hattie Sharpe. We're meant to meet here while Everland Theater is wrapped up with construction tape."

I offered him a fake smile. "Well, you're welcome to hang out. Browse some movies." Panic gripped my throat. What the heck was I going to tell him when Hattie returned? That I'd lied about who I was? For now, it felt safe, but if I was wrong about him...

"Thank you. Hattie is usually prompt with our phone calls and mail exchanges, so I'm surprised she isn't here."

He sauntered to the right, casually glancing over the wall of candy. I'd never seen a vampire show any interest in food. They only drank synthetic blood. Or real blood. I reached for my bottle of Pepsi, eyeing it for a moment as the seed of an idea formed.

Rufus shuffled into the aisle of horror films. That section had been getting a lot of action lately. More than the action movies, anyway. He plucked *Interview with the Vampire* off the shelf and snorted. I lifted my wolf ears and turned them forward to catch what he muttered under his breath.

"Derivative."

He wasn't wrong. Anne Rice wrote the book well before Tom Cruise performed in the movie version.

"How does this crap get traction?" he seethed.

I didn't love the irritation in his voice or the choking stench of smoke that came with it, and I definitely didn't agree that *Interview with the Vampire* was crap.

I took a swig of soda and slammed the bottle down on the desk, summoning a loud voice. "Excuse me," I said, catching his attention again. His amethyst eyes were sharp as they pinned me. As much as I had relished these past quiet months of security in Bewitcher's Beach, I found myself more on edge around a potential killer than ever before. Something about this entire situation was different than the other murderers I'd investigated. The healing bite marks on my arm suddenly itched something fierce. I resisted the urge to claw at the wounds. Rubbing my palm over the itchiness, I faked another smile as I spoke. "Can I get you anything while you wait? Maybe a bottle of YumBlood?"

I glanced at the little black refrigerator next to the wall of candy. Hopefully, I had a YumBlood crammed in there some-where between the sodas.

His mouth lifted in a lifeless half-smile. "No, thank you."

"Another brand? I can run to the grocery next door." I really wanted to duck out of here. This nervous energy defi-nitely came from the bat's attack. The bite wounds prickled at my tender flesh, and I itched to scratch and scratch and scratch.

"I'm not thirsty, thank you."

"Are you sure?" Now I was truly committed to getting the heck of out of here. If I couldn't find relief by scratching at the bites, I wanted a breath of fresh air.

"I'm sure."

"Don't you drink synthetic blood?" I didn't mean to say it out loud. I really didn't, but nerves had a way of twisting my tongue and that darn itching hijacked my brain.

The cat-like slits in his purple eyes narrowed. My pulse thumped, and I expected to drop to all fours any second now, but my energy was sapped by this load of nerves and the amount of focus it took to not scratch at the scabs.

His tongue darted out over his lips. "Of course I drink synthetic blood."

The smell of heavy smoke filled my nose. Rufus was irritated by my insinuation. Vampires weren't supposed to drink real blood anymore, not even from blood donations, and not while we supernaturals were still trying to find our place out in the open.

The burn of the smoky scent carried notes of week-old sushi. Stinky, rotten fish revealed liars every single time. Rufus definitely felt guilty about something, and I was willing to bet it had to do with his claim.

He didn't drink synthetic blood at all. He drank Ryan's blood, and maybe he'd intended to drink mine...

But how would killing me stop construction and save him

money? And he'd shown no surprise when I claimed to be Ms. Titan, though that didn't prove he didn't already know my identity. He spent his life surrounded by brilliant actors, and I had no doubt he'd picked up a few tricks of the trade.

Maybe he hoped any death related to the project would end it. Maybe without me, he thought Hattie would drop the dream of transforming Everland Theater and then he'd have no problem pulling his funding.

If Rufus was the killer, he'd already attacked me once, as a bat, which meant he'd have no qualms with doing it again.

I wanted to shrink back to the phone on the wall, but calling Sett was useless, so instead, I faced the situation head on and intended to smell for his next lie.

"Is this your first time in Mockbuster?" I asked.

His head slowly swiveled back to me. "Yes, I'm visiting the town with my wife."

I couldn't pinpoint any guilt in his emotions, but that could be because of the latter half of his comment. He was here with his wife. That wasn't a lie at all.

"How long have you been in town?" That'd give me a reference.

"We just arrived yesterday."

I nodded and hummed as if interested in his travel details. Adrenaline buzzed in my veins from the moment I smelled his lie. My energy was slowly returning, which meant I could finally defend myself if I needed to.

Rufus took two strides forward, eyeing me as he stopped right at the spot where Ryan's body had lain. It sickened me to think Rufus might have returned to the scene of the crime, and a crime he'd caused all to save himself money. If he was, in fact, the killer.

I wasn't sure of anything, but Hattie knew him better and she'd suggested our patron could be the murderer.

"Are you looking forward to Everland Theater playing your films?" I asked.

His eyes narrowed. A nauseating mix of smells sloughed off of him with a dozen different emotions. "When did I say that?" His tongue darted out again as he took a step toward me. "You are Ms. Wolf, aren't you? Hattie said to look for a curly-haired wolf who runs the video shop."

"I have a few names."

He sucked air through his teeth. "Why didn't you say that before? We can get this meeting started now."

"We should wait for Hattie."

Shaking his head, he nearly spoke over me. "No time to waste. I'm ready to get down to business. My wife is already ticked off at me for spending half our date doing business. I promised her this meeting would be short. Now, these are the facts, Ms. Wolf. I'm pulling the funding, and I'd like you two to keep it quiet."

"Excuse me?"

"I said, you need to keep it quiet. I pledged a lot of money to this project, and I can't have another thing fail publicly."

It felt like a fire had suddenly ignited between us and the smoke was billowing out in great puffs. The smell choked in my nose and throat. His anger and impatience whittled away at my courage as he continued.

"I'd like you and Hattie to say that you took the money and used it for something else."

"That's a lie."

"So lie. It's Hollywood, Ms. Wolf. Acting is the business of lies."

I recoiled. The itch of the wound faded, but the urge to shift into my wolf form overwhelmed me. I tried resisting, but that didn't stop my claws from extending. I folded them behind my back to keep my defensive nerves hidden. "And why would we do this?" Another question that slipped out. Why would I ask that? He'd probably just kill us if we didn't agree.

Rufus splayed his hands on the desk, his long fingernails scratching at the top. My stomach twisted. "I'm a very powerful man, Ms. Wolf."

I shuffled to the side of the desk, putting distance between us because the flimsy wooden desk wasn't enough protection. "You can't threaten me."

"Just stick to the plan."

"And if I don't?"

His fingers curled into a fist and he slammed it against the desk.

That was enough to push me over the edge. Fur sprang out over my skin, and in a flash, I was all animal. I growled and bared my teeth up at him in a warning to get out of my shop, but Rufus could shift just as fast.

As soon as the rumble built in my chest, his cloak billowed to the floor, empty and lifeless as his human form vanished. The cape quickly followed—which proved this was Chanel's design. An enchanted cape that could cease to exist when the wearer was in their shifter form. Once he became a vampire again, it'd simply reappear on his body.

As a bat, he flickered above me, his purple eyes now red and his movements too erratic and quick for me to follow.

Rufus dropped down at me, his leathery wings flapping. I snapped at the air, but I was too slow. He was small, jittery, and a fast moving-target as he swooped for my neck.

Once again, he got to me. Rufus, in bat form, bit me as hard as he could. He sank his tiny, needle fangs into my neck, and if I didn't get him off of me, he might bleed me dry.

CHAPTER 10
SAFETY IN NUMBERS

THE BITE LASTED NO MORE than ten seconds, but it left me somewhere between dizzy and fired up. Rufus fluttered away from me and snapped back into his human form, where the cloak modestly covered him. He ducked toward the front door, fully covered and fully vampire now.

I shook off the stinging pain of the bite but did not let him leave without a growl and a snap at the air. Before he made it to the door, I lunged for him, my jaws open wide to grab his arm and prevent him from leaving. There was no way I would let him run off after attacking me again.

But Rufus was a strong vampire, stronger than my werewolf self, which was all the power I could muster. He ripped away from me, yanked the door open, and darted outside. I slipped through the door before it fell shut, but he'd already vanished once my paws hit the pavement.

Rufus had attacked me again, and disappeared.

I huffed and licked my snout. The bite didn't hurt like last time, not with the thick fur blocking him from sinking his fangs too deep. My werewolf form had saved me, but that didn't stop the disturbed shiver that slithered over my neck. I shook out my ears and darted across town to the station.

Sett wouldn't understand my barks, but I needed him to go after Rufus right now. Waiting until I could shift back and get dressed only gave him time to escape. Hattie would have to put the message together through my barks and whines. She'd done it for me before, and sure enough, once I arrived at the station, Hattie pieced the information together based on the bite in my neck and that she'd left me alone with Rufus the vampire.

Armed with information, Sett made a plan to track Rufus down before he dodged town. Surely, the vampire movie director and his wife would grab their bags at the hotel before leaving. We'd meet there as soon as I could transform back into my human self and throw on some clothes.

That was how I ended up striding into The Oyster Inn only twenty minutes after running to the police station. Hattie stayed back to watch Everland Theater in case Rufus showed up while I went marching into the inn on two legs. Of course Sett had beat me there since I had to make a detour, transform back, and slip into a pair of jeans and a T-shirt.

A decadent chandelier and shiny floors mismatched the quaint and homey outside of the inn. Such elegant decor wasn't unusual for a fairy, and Barney kept to the standard. Running The Oyster Inn meant he could design every nook and cranny after the fairy realm. Here in Bewitcher's Beach, he was just a grumpy old human-looking guy in a beige sweater, but I knew the decor made him feel like he was home.

Barney's jowls quivered as he shook his head, presumably answering one of Sett's questions. Sett's back was to me as I marched up to the reception desk. My tattered sneakers clopped against the marble, and Sett swiveled at my approach.

"Rufus already left," he said.

"Like packed up and checked out?" I glanced between him and Barney.

Barney blinked at me lazily. "If a guest has somewhere to be, I'm not one to stand in their way. He paid up and they scuttled off like two kids on a honeymoon."

Ignoring Barney's inaccurate description of Rufus being like a "kid," I turned to Sett. The hard lines of his stony face were softened with concern, but Sett was never too soft. The rigid rule-follower inside always showed through, it was the perfect balance for his job. Soft with a child whose toy had been stolen, hard against criminals.

"Do you think he's already out of town?" I asked.

"I think it's going to be tricky to track him down, but I'll find him. In the meantime, I want you to stick with me."

I tilted my head, and he hurried to explain. "For safety. Or you can stick with Crow. I'd just rather you not be alone, despite what Hattie says. You can defend yourself just fine, but I'd rather you have..." His voice trailed off.

I smirked. "Backup?"

He reached out, giving my shoulder a gentle squeeze. "Two is better than one."

"I'll have Hattie stick with me."

His voice turned gravelly, and his brow tipped forward. "Is Crow gone again?"

My mouth popped open in surprise. With how news traveled in Bewitcher's Beach, I expected he'd already found out somehow. Either Hattie had mentioned it, or Cordelia, who served us the Breakup Milkshake.

I shook the shock off my face. "Whatever Crow has decided to do today isn't exactly my business." That was the best way I could think to put it for now. Discussing my breakup at a time like this not only felt like a distraction from finding Rufus but also disrespectful to the deceased, whose loved ones deserved answers.

My love life was the least important part of today's equation. Though the searing stare in Sett's gray eyes said otherwise.

I looked away before the heat building in my neck was evident across my cheeks. "I'll have Hattie go to the doctor with me."

It was Sett's turn to go slack-jawed. After a moment, he smiled. "I wasn't going to say anything about you needing to see Doctor Pitt."

"Sure."

"I wasn't."

"Uh huh."

"Noema."

"Sett, I know how controlling you are." I dabbed the soft pad of my fingers against the red marks of the bite. They had stopped bleeding almost immediately since the bite wasn't deep, but the skin still swelled and felt sore to the touch.

"Controlling?"

I shrugged. "In a concerned way."

He leaned closer, as if he didn't want Barney overhearing our conversation. Though Barney paid us no attention as he went back to polishing the crystal lamp that sat on the reception desk.

Sett's breath smelled of cinnamon with a hint of nutty coffee. I tried to pick out the emotional scents beneath his breakfast, but Sett had always been harder to read for me. After a moment, I only pinpointed minty curiosity. Was it about the investigation? Or did he want to know more about my breakup?

"I think the word you were looking for is protective," he said. The curl of his mouth suggested he was hoping I'd agree. "Don't you know that's what police officers do?"

"Hmm, I didn't think police officers took care of animal bites."

"If that animal is a criminal..."

I snapped my fingers and shot him a finger gun. "Touche."

"Let me walk you to the clinic," he said as we made our way to the door. Barney didn't bid us goodbye as we slipped out onto the sidewalk.

Outside, I paused. "I can see if Hattie will accompany me since you have to track Rufus down." I threw my thumb over my shoulder at the theater across the alley.

"No need." Sett turned and palmed my back. Nodding across town toward the clinic, he gently prodded me along. "Protection first, investigation second. And Hattie has her own job watching to see if Rufus returns to demand his money."

That was a good point, but it was more about if Hattie would lie for him about the money. Rufus cared about his reputation first. Though after killing Ryan and attacking me, what was his reputation worth? He'd have to go into hiding, or Sett and the other police officers would snag him. What did that mean for the future of supernatural films? And more importantly, for the future of Everland Theater?

We'd either have to find a new patron or move on from this dream.

We walked side-by-side, with just enough respectable distance so Chanel and Co wouldn't assume I'd already moved on from Crow.

"Are you okay?" Sett asked. "You've been through a lot lately with the..." He stopped. With the breakup? With the attacks? He sighed and scrubbed at the back of his neck. "I don't want to overstep, or be...controlling." He winced as if the word physically hurt him. It was no secret that Sett was controlling, even beyond his job's duties, but maybe he wasn't as prone to it as he used to be. Maybe he was working on it, and

I hadn't noticed since I'd spent the past few months dodging his path. Despite all my avoidance, it somehow appeared as if I'd had two boyfriends. As if I'd played with the emotions of two men. I mirrored his wince, and he didn't miss it. Sett frowned and continued. "This is coming from Officer Lawrence. I have to do my job and recommend that you and the kids should stay at Mae and Wallace's until I have Mr. Harrington in custody."

The sweet smell of his coffee faded as I finally drew in the scent of his emotions. Guilt always turned my stomach. Though it usually smelled of rotten fish, the flavors of guilt were like the shades of gray in Sett's eyes. Each shade, or reason for the emotion, was different even though it pointed to the same feeling. Sett wasn't lying or hiding anything. I didn't think Sett even had the capacity to lie. This spoiled-milk-smelling guilt came directly from his words. He had to tell me what to do even though he knew I didn't like it. I wasn't exactly the type of wolf who listened, even if my ears caught every sound.

My heart skipped. Sett shouldn't have to feel guilt when he was only trying to protect me. I'd shirked him off before, and it was true he'd overstepped in the past a few times, but he'd invited me into the investigation this time.

"I still can't believe you didn't insist that I go see the doctor," I said as we stopped in front of the clinic.

"What?"

"You knew I'd been bitten again, but you didn't insist I come here before helping to look for Rufus."

"Last time you were attacked, you let me carry you here instead of arguing. You've never let me help so easily before. I figured if you were really hurt, you wouldn't ignore it."

Maybe we'd both changed a little. I didn't yell at him to put me down. Sure, I'd been about to faint, but in the past, the threat of fainting wouldn't have stopped me from insisting on fierce independence.

Since Christopher died, leaving me with four children to care for on my own, I'd developed a need to do *everything* on my own. Even walk myself to the clinic. But Sett was right about last time; I'd let him carry me. I'd accepted help without overthinking it. The pain may have pushed it the first time, but here I was again, letting him walk me to the clinic and not even itching to argue about my need for a "buddy system" of safety.

I didn't want to run around Bewitcher's Beach alone after two attacks. I think I actually wanted a little help.

"Thank you," I said with a small smile.

"Anytime. Call me if you can't find anyone else to accompany you when you leave the clinic."

"I meant, thank you for being protective, and I'm sorry I called you controlling. It's been a weird couple of days." Not that that excused my behavior.

"I am controlling at times," he said.

"Because of your job?" I didn't know why I asked it until Sett winced again. I'd never been able to smell his emotions in the past, but I slowly developed a skill to soak in the scent from beneath his hard outer shell, and since then, his emotions had been hard to pinpoint. Sett knew everything about everybody in town, but I got the feeling I didn't know as much about him.

"Because people have died when I've been too agreeable." With that, he offered me a sad smile and stepped past me. "Will you call me from the clinic's phone if you have to walk out alone?"

"I'll call for backup."

I caught the flickering scent of key lime pie. Maybe I smelled my own hope. Hope for safety, hope for our friendship to return now that I didn't have to avoid him.

But when I turned and slipped inside the clinic, the sweetness of key lime pie vanished. Dread promptly overpowered it as I took in the sterile smell of the doctor's office. I unlovingly called the stench of dread "pee toast" since it was a mixture of fear's ammonia and the burnt bread of regret.

I hated shots.

CHAPTER 11
RED RINGS

DOCTOR PITT'S voice droned on about how it was helpful that I'd already had the rabies vaccine. According to the doctor's explanation, a vampire who shifted into a bat could carry rabies but would never get it as an undead person. Since I was bitten while he was in bat form, I would have been at risk.

Thankfully, I didn't need another shot so soon.

"Would I have been at risk even if he didn't break skin?"

"He broke the skin." Doctor Pitt spoke matter-of-factly, but he always had a hint of nervousness around him. It made for terrible bedside manner, but his nurses claimed he was the best doctor they'd ever worked for because his nerves had him researching excessively. His cautiousness saved lives.

People have died when I'm too agreeable. I mused over Sett's declaration. When did this happen? I couldn't remember a time when he was lenient on any laws that resulted in someone's demise. Whatever he was referring to wasn't an event that'd happened any time in the last several years. And before that, Bewitcher's Beach was shielded by the witch's protection spell. Nobody died other than from old age, and people very rarely got hurt.

"I didn't bleed much," I said, hoping that was enough to avoid any other shots Doctor Pitt might have recommended. "And the bites are tiny."

"Tiny or not, it can transmit diseases."

"So if he'd bitten me when he wasn't a bat..."

"You wouldn't have needed a rabies vaccine. But I still recommend an antibiotic injection to help protect this bite from infection since you were in wolf form when it happened and your fur could have gotten a little dirt or dust into the wounds."

I knew there'd be another shot coming. I folded my arms and grunted, basically copying Stevie's pouting. As a grown woman, I shouldn't be whining, but nobody other than Doctor Pitt was around to witness it, and the doctor never judged anybody.

Doctor Pitt filled a syringe from a small bottle and then flicked it, knocking air bubbles to the top. Pushing a small stream out, he readied the shot to go into my veins.

I frowned and braced for the needle to break the skin. "I'd rather have a vampire bite than a shot," I muttered.

He snorted. "I've heard those hurt far more than a shot. Plus, the red rings around the bites stay for months after."

"Red rings?" I squinted at him. From what I remembered, Ryan's throat looked like clay with two colorless holes poked through.

"Yes, immediately after puncture, red rings form and rise up like swollen circles around the bite."

"Weird," I said, thinking aloud. "Ryan didn't have that, and he was bled dry by a vampire."

"It wasn't a vampire, then." He shook his head as he focused the tip of the needle at the edge of my skin. The soft flesh gave way around the needle, and I sucked in a sharp breath. In a second, it was over, and he was popping a fluffy cotton ball out of a glass jar. Stretching a piece of brown tape over it, he secured the cotton ball to my arm, and I swallowed the stench of dread in my throat. Peeling that off with my arm hair later was basically salt on the wound.

Before he could jump up and send the nurses in, I met his gaze. "Are you sure every vampire bite causes red rings?"

He snapped off his gloves and tossed them into a trash can beside a small sink and counter, then pumped several drops of soap into his palm. "As positive as O positive." He chuckled at his blood joke. "Vampires never fail to leave a red ring when they bite and suck blood while in their vampire form. It lasts for months after the bite."

"What if the person is no longer alive?"

He popped his lips. "Well, if they're drained of blood, the swelling and redness go away, but it leaves a white ring on skin for up to a year."

"Is it from infection?"

"Oh no, it's because blood is drawn out so fast. It forms to completely stop the bleeding on anyone alive or recently dead."

"Would a bitten person still bleed an hour or so after?"

He shook his head. "Not a drop. The red rings collect any leftover blood beneath the skin."

Ryan was definitely still bleeding, though it wasn't much. "That's so weird," I mused.

"It happens because vampires don't want to waste any blood. Of course, I mean when vampires still drank blood. YumBlood is truly a miracle. I can't imagine how awful it must have been to feel hunger and have to attack people to stop it." A nervous shake vibrated in his voice, though I smelled no ammonia. Doctor Pitt was forever a nervous guy, but the scent of lavender poking through the sterile environment ensured he was telling the truth. "I'll send my nurse to get you a box of juice, and then you'll be free to leave if you're feeling steady enough to stand."

I nodded, though I only heard half of what he'd said after juice. The bite on Ryan's neck looked nothing like the vampire bites Doctor Pitt explained.

Why didn't Bart say anything about this when he examined Ryan's body? Was Bart's retirement throwing off his skill as a coroner? Was Ryan bitten while Rufus was in his bat form? I didn't know if any of that mattered, but it felt worth looking into.

I sucked down my box of apple juice before rolling off the plastic bed and ducking out of the doctor's office.

The best part about living in a small town was that the lab the coroner worked out of was right behind the clinic. It took no more than two minutes to stride across the cobblestone and knock on Bart's door. The bad part about living in a small town was that eighty percent of the time, people weren't at their places of business, unless those places of business were the tourist shops.

Here, you could work odd hours and only the gossips would complain while the rest of us appreciated the flexible lifestyle in the bubble of Bewitcher's Beach. I knocked and knocked but to no avail. I'd have to pop over to Bart's house and ask him about what he may have missed during Ryan's examination.

Of course, Sett wouldn't want me to go alone, and if I was honest with myself, I didn't even like being alone now either. Rufus was on the run with a sun-shielding cape. For all I knew, he was lurking in the alley behind the clinic or any of the other nearby buildings.

So I stalked off toward the closest and safest place I could think of: the police station. But that too was empty and locked up. My next option was Roller Shakes, but I didn't think showing my face at Crow's business was fair just yet. Our breakup was too fresh, and even though it was amicable, mutual even, the thought of seeing all the little reminders of him around the rink did unsettling things to my stomach. We weren't ready to be friends yet, that much I knew.

And truthfully, the change was enough to set my nerves on edge. I'd never dealt with change smoothly, not after Christopher's death, or even before. Maybe my sudden and mysterious shift from being a simple witch to turning into a werewolf had something to do with it.

Hair prickled on the back of my neck, rising as if to warn me that someone's eyes were on me. I whipped around. Scanning the alley between the clinic and the lab, I found nothing odd. Nobody was around, and the shades on the windows were drawn, so I knew nobody was peering out of the clinic at me.

My wolf ears perked, catching the faint clop of footsteps. My gaze whipped toward the alley's dead end. Beyond the end of the cobblestone, there were thick trees and shrubbery. Past that was the beach.

This alley wasn't used often since Bart had retired and the nurses and patients used the front door of the clinic. The shrubbery was too thick to blaze a shortcut to the beach. Whoever was back here was either coming to the coroner's lab or following me.

"Bart?" I said.

The footsteps on the other side of the clinic faded. A yawning shadow went with it. I blew out a breath and darted to the other side of the clinic. If it was Bart, he would have responded. I needed to get out of this lonely place and back to where people could see me. Being alone never my intention.

I hurried to the front of the clinic, finally taking a full breath when I spotted joggers in the park. Shoppers lingered outside of Chanel's boutique while cars on the road beeped at one another.

I scanned the street to see if anyone was walking particularly fast—someone in a cloak. But I only saw the reaper who ran the workout studio and two of her clients moving fast. They jogged along the sidewalk and past the boutique.

The sidewalk was packed with people. Chanel stopped chatting with a decadently dressed couple to watch a man saunter by. He tipped his cap to her and kept going. Behind me, three men loitered outside Roller Shakes with soda cups in hand as they loudly argued over some sports team's statistics.

And right there, flitting past the three men, were two leathery wings. There was no way I could chase after a flying creature. Well, sure, I could chase Rufus as a bat, but I wouldn't catch him.

The bat disappeared beyond Roller Shakes and into the shadow of the forest behind the parking lot.

Even though I recognized a friendly face or two—I wasn't alone—I scurried across town as fast as I could go on two legs. I'd shifted enough for one day, and since I wasn't in immediate danger, I figured keeping my clothes on was the best choice.

At Mockbuster, I gave Sett a call to let him know what I'd learned about vampire bites. Even he wouldn't know since vampires biting people was something of the long ago past.

When he didn't answer, I left a message on his answering machine. I requested for him to return my call ASAP and left him a promise that I'd be with Hattie for the rest of the day.

A promise I kept.

She haunted me at the shop, and to summer camp pickup, and then back at the loft, since Rufus never showed up to claim his money or threaten her.

When the kids, Hattie, and I all sat down to watch the only new release VHS copy of *The Quest for Camelot* I had in stock, I finally peeled the cotton ball and tape off my arm in one swift rip. I slapped my hand against the spot where it tore out tiny hairs and rubbed my palm over it until the stinging subsided.

"Was that the worst part of your day, Mommy?" Stevie asked, peering at me from where she was buried in pillows on the corner of the couch.

"Hmm, maybe," I said, thinking back to the attack and the shot. The worst part would be if I didn't hear from Sett at all. He hadn't returned my call, which either meant that he'd caught Rufus's trail and was busy contacting other officers in nearby towns to help track him down, or he only had bad news and didn't want to have to tell me.

I scooted closer to Stevie and wrapped my arm around her. Pulling her in for a squeeze, I stole a few pieces of popcorn from the bowl in her lap. "What about you? Did the gym teacher tell you to focus again?"

She shook her head so eagerly I thought it might fly right off her shoulders. "No, but guess what?"

"What?"

"He broke his back too!"

"Seriously?"

Jovi shook his head from where he perched on the arm of the couch behind Stevie. "He was just sick."

"Whatever." Stevie rolled her eyes, tired of Jovi always correcting her imaginative details.

"Mrs. B let us play dodgeball!" Dio shouted entirely too loudly for a casual conversation in our tiny loft. "I whopped Halen's whole team. Didn't I, Halen? Tell Mom."

Halen ignored him as he shoveled popcorn into his mouth and soaked up every second of the new movie. His eyes and ears may as well have been glued to the TV screen.

Hattie shifted her eyes from Halen to me. "This kid sure

knows how to drown out a bad day. Maybe we should take a lesson from him."

I forced a grim smile. Today was truly awful, but at least the killer was no longer a mystery. We had a name and a face for the person who'd ended Ryan's life. Now that he'd exposed himself by attacking me in the same way he'd attacked Ryan, he'd be investigated and arrested.

We wouldn't have to lie for him. But we would have to find a new patron and start over with Everland Theater's transformation if we ever wanted to give supernatural people access to the movies.

Good things took time, and really, maybe I needed more time to accept another change in Bewitcher's Beach.

CHAPTER 12
WAITING

BETWEEN TRACKING RUFUS—OR attempting to—and Sett's other duties as the sheriff of Bewitcher's Beach, he was swamped, and I was forced to wait patiently.

Doctor Pitt's information about the vampire bite didn't sway Sett's schedule. Not with the fall festival approaching and Sett determined to squash the rise of petty crime before the annual event. Bart was a skilled coroner, and Sett was already busy looking for a major suspect.

But the details nagged at me. Why didn't Ryan's bite look right? I wouldn't find out until Sett had time to accompany me to Bart's house.

I hated waiting, but I'd developed my skill for it over the past few months thanks to several slow processes.

Waiting for the witches at Shadowvale to recreate the protection spell. Waiting to find out if those same witches found anything in The Book of Prophecies that could lead me to my missing family. Waiting for Crow to call me. Waiting for a patron to sponsor Everland Theater's transformation.

But when the transformation came, I wasn't even ready. Would I be ready if I ever found the Titan family? It was a fifty-fifty guess. When it came to Crow and our relationship, I was definitely ready for the end. The distance between us these past few months, both physical and emotional, set us up for an easy separation. And if nothing else, at least the breakup gave me a little practice accepting change.

Though I'd yet to incorporate anything new in my routine.

I still woke up this morning and followed my same old schedule for the past three days. Dropping the kids off, organizing the rentals in the return bin, booting up the old computer at exactly 9:50 in the morning so that it'd be done loading and working as Mockbuster's register by the ten o' clock open time. And all while sipping on a Diet Pepsi.

The only deviation from my routine was unplugging my at-home VCR and moving it down to the shop to play videos throughout the day. I popped *Under Wraps* into the VCR to bring a little background noise into the shop.

I could easily shake up this routine if I wasn't so busy. I'd done it many times before. Sometimes I went for a wolf run on the beach before opening the shop. Other days I taped a sign to the shop's door and let the kids play hooky from school so we could watch movies all day.

But it didn't matter how spontaneously I approached everyday life. All those little adventures hadn't prepared me for the big changes, like watching Everland Theater's stage get ripped out, or Bewitcher's Beach becoming so crowded that dozens of unfamiliar faces passed through my shop everyday.

The phone trilled as customers called asking about hours. As soon as I slipped away from the phone and unlocked the door, people piled in.

I should appreciate the rush of customers as of late, but overwhelm got to me. For the past two days, the amount of people swinging through Mockbuster's door doubled, and then doubled again. I couldn't keep the carpet vacuumed. I couldn't keep the wall of candy stocked. And the new releases wall? Empty.

This made for a few angry customers too.

I downed the dregs of my soda as a witch with a signature crystal tattoo and a furrowed brow stormed up to the desk. Her long black fingernails clattered against the desktop as she smacked her palms down against it. My heart leaped into my throat, and I instinctively drew back, bumping my butt against the stool I hadn't had time to sit on.

The witch leaned her button nose closer to me, and my pulse ticked up. This was entirely too much like Rufus's attack.

"I was told this place is always stocked," she snapped. The phone rang again, but I ignored it to give this woman my full attention.

"The new releases are going fast—"

"You don't even have *Hocus Pocus*," she interrupted. "And it's a five-year-old movie."

I tried not to twist my face at the stench of her anger, but her emotions burned in my nose until a sneeze burst out of me. I wiped my nose and apologized. "I can take down your phone number and give you a call when the next copy returns."

"I'm leaving town tomorrow," she said. "Will it be in before tomorrow? I need something to do while my boyfriend is stuck here. Help."

"Uh, can I recommend something else? *The Craft* is good."

She groaned and dropped her head back like I'd seen Bette do many times when Hattie lectured her. "Fine. Whatever. Can't do anything else."

The bell chimed, and three more people walked in, crowding the small shop with almost twenty customers, and on a Thursday afternoon at that. This was wild, but the money would come in handy.

I popped around the desk, squeezed through a group of

people chatting in a circle by the candy wall, and grabbed the VHS for *The Craft*. Returning to the register, I scanned it and offered the witch a polite smile. "If you finish this and still have time to kill, the beach is nice at this time of year before fall really hits and it gets cold."

She pointed a spiky black fingernail at the windows. "You mean the human sand pit? I couldn't even find a spot to put down my towel."

Oof. Had it gotten that bad?

One look at my shop confirmed it. No wonder Sett was busy. He likely had a heap of cars to pull over for speeding, fines to dole out for littering, and a dozen other minor infractions that quadrupled every time we experienced an influx of tourists.

I sucked in a breath as I handed her the video tape. "Maybe a nice walk around the park?"

"Funny." She rolled her eyes. "Last time I did that, a creepy dude followed me around just to call me a freak and tell me that my magic should be outlawed. Like, I thought this was a haven for supernatural people, you know? Ugh."

She didn't give me a chance to defend Bewitcher's Beach, and I didn't know if I even should. If some guy harassed her, Sett ought to know, especially since hunters often used the word "freak" to describe supernatural people.

The witch already turned away from me and another customer approached, but I raised my voice to shout over the incessant ring of the phone on the wall behind my head. Before she shoved through the door, I called out, "You should run that by the sheriff!"

She swiveled, her glossy white-blond pixie cut ruffling with the gust of wind from the open door. "Done and done."

I nodded and faced an endless line of customers for the next hour. A couple stepped up with two armfuls of horror movies. A mother and daughter rented *Jumani*, and the man behind them dropped *Goodfellas* on the desk.

"Busy shop," he said, his pale blue eyes darting from the candy wall to the TV behind my head. "Summer keeping you on your toes?"

I nodded. "Something like that."

"Does it ever get quiet in here?"

I met his gaze now and hummed. "Lately? Not often."

"What time does it slow down?"

"After seven in the evening," I said. "By then, everyone is home watching their rentals."

He accepted the video tape back from me. "Rad. I'll keep that in mind for next time. I'm not a fan of crowds." I couldn't blame him. I wasn't loving the sardine feeling either. Bewitcher's Beach just wasn't big enough to support this many people. The man lifted his tape as he turned toward the door. "Anyway, thanks."

Mae shared a similar sentiment as she marched up to the desk after him. "I'm with the coach; this is too much. I can't even keep track of who is who on my morning walks with Wallace anymore. Though I have to say, the challenge of all the new names and faces is doing my memory good. They say that you should do puzzles and games to keep your mind sharp as you age. I could tell you almost every name of the people who're in here."

"Oh yeah?" I smiled at Mae. Relief relaxed my shoulders, because even if she rambled on and maybe irritated the customers in line behind her, I soaked up this familiar moment. She was a friendly face, not an angry tourist.

"Sally and Janice are a lovely couple visiting from Portland. Dylan is a looker with those biceps. But if you ask me, he shouldn't have shaved his head. Tammy is considering retiring here if she can convince her husband to live with a bunch of supernatural people." She lowered her voice, which didn't actually change the volume at all but gave her a raspy sound. "Apparently, he's scared of vampires after the whole"—her bright eyes flickered to the floor—"you know?"

I snorted. As long as this lady's husband didn't mess with Rufus's reputation or money, he didn't have anything to worry about.

"Oh, and I was just with Sett," Mae continued. "He tried to give you a call a few times, but you didn't answer. He said I'm a more reliable form of communication than a phone." Mae beamed at that, her cheeks rosy. I knew Sett well enough to know his comment was a simple matter-of-fact, but to Mae, this was the highest compliment. "If you can get away, he wants you to meet him at the coroner's lab at one-thirty this afternoon."

I straightened my spine, and the tall posture seemed to lift my mood. Finally, I didn't have to wait and wonder why Ryan's bite marks felt so off.

And finally, I had an excuse to get out of here and breathe.

CHAPTER 13
THE TRUTH COMES OUT

HAVING RAKED in three times the amount of money Mockbuster made on a usual Thursday morning, I closed the doors to take a late lunch break out of the building. At least, that was what the note taped on the inside of the glass door said.

Nobody could fault me for needing food, right? Wrong. Angry customers faulted employees for anything and everything, so maybe that was wishful thinking.

But the tourist's irritation was a problem for future Noema. I prepared a spiel for the first person who complained about my business's odd hours as I hurried across town.

A line of customers clamored outside of Roller Shakes. More people piled into Chanel's boutique, the taffy shop, and the other small stores that lined the beach side of town. Cars honked at one another and circled the town, enjoying the views with the hood of their convertible vehicles pulled down.

The hair on the back of my neck prickled, and I got the odd feeling that they were viewing me, like a hunter stalking his prey. Or maybe the driver simply couldn't find a spot to park, and they hoped I was walking to my car. I pushed the crosswalk button and waited to cross the street to where Roller Shakes and the police station sat on the other side.

When the crosswalk signal beeped a friendly tune, I skipped into the road. The sudden roar of an engine sent my pulse crowding my throat. I snapped my head toward the oncoming sports car. I had the right of way, but the flaming red car didn't stop—it sped up.

My heart sprang into my throat as the corvette barreled at me. It seemed the driver hit the gas as soon as I stepped into the crosswalk. I bolted to the other side of the crosswalk, feeling the front bumper clip the back of my shoe. Yelping, I spun around to shoot the driver a glare, but I only caught the back of a man's head as he roared the engine and sped off past the clinic.

Every limb in my body was still shaking from the close call when I rounded the clinic and caught sight of Sett at the door to the lab. He stopped checking his watch and looked up as I approached.

He opened his mouth, but it quickly turned to a frown. "Are you okay?"

"I've seen a ghost," I joked as I threw my thumb over my shoulder. "Somebody was driving too fast at the crosswalk. Red corvette. Have you seen them?"

He sighed. "I've given a few tickets out this week but not to a corvette. I'll keep a sharper eye on the roads."

"You're busy enough. You need to bring another officer into the station."

"I would. If I had time to hire someone."

Poor Sett had a bad taste in his mouth when it came to hiring a partner. His last hire turned out to be his ex-girlfriend, who also turned out to be a murderer. Not a single soul could blame his hesitance.

As soon as Bart opened the door and welcomed us into the lab, a horrible burst of ammonia struck me. I swallowed the sickness rising in my throat. Was this how the lab always smelled?

Much to my nose's dismay, we stepped inside, where Bart had Ryan's body displayed on a steel table. The space was small, crowded with the lab equipment and the wall of cold cabinets that doubled as the town's mortuary. At least the constant blast of air conditioning kept the room chilly enough for me.

Bart sniffed and palmed at his wild hair. "Here he is."

I blinked and squinted at the holes in Ryan's neck. I wrinkled my nose at the sight of his colorless skin where it was bare of anything other than two small holes. No red rings, no white circles. I glanced at Sett, who slid his gaze to Bart.

"I appreciate you taking the time to examine the victim again," Sett said. "We have reason to believe the attack might not be vampiric in nature."

Bart stiffened. I shot Sett another glance. Sniffing carefully, I pinpointed the odor of Bart's ammonia against the sterile smell of the lab. What did he have to be afraid of?

Sett took the initiative on the examination, crouching before the table to look over the bites. He grabbed a blue glove from a box on a nearby counter and snapped it on. Touching the bites gently, he rubbed his finger over the surrounding area. "I don't feel any bumps or see anything other than the holes."

"Did you see any red rings around the bite when you first looked at him?" I asked Bart. "I couldn't remember seeing any, but of course I didn't examine him like you did."

Bart shook his head. "Red rings? Red rings..." He stared blankly at the body. "Red rings."

"From what I understand, vampire bites always leave a raised red circle that can turn white later on," I repeated what Doctor Pitt had taught me.

The wispy hairs protruding from the top of Bart's head rose and fell with his eager nod. "That's true. That's true."

"Is it true that maybe Ryan wasn't killed by a vampire?" Sett asked as he popped back to his feet and peeled the glove off.

The ammonia grew stronger, beckoning rotten fish along with the sickening smell. Bart was as scared as he was guilty. But he was already retired, which meant he couldn't lose his job. What did Bart have to be afraid of if he'd made an honest mistake and misread Ryan's cause of death? Of course, the guilt suggested something worse than a simple mistake.

"Bart?" Sett prodded gently.

His eyes bugged out as they darted back and forth between Sett and me and then dropped to Ryan again. "I–I–I can't say."

Sett's voice was soft when he spoke again. "Bart, I know you. You've never made a mistake. Nobody will fault you for a slip up. But I'm willing to bet that's not the case because you're as sharp as your autopsy tools. So tell me, what's really going on?"

"They—" Bart's throat bobbed in a long swallow. "They came to me in a mask."

"They?" Sett guided him to keep talking.

"Just one," he said. "I don't know if this person was a man or a woman because they wore one of those nude lady leggings over their head. Their face was all distorted, and a hat covered their hair. They didn't speak. They didn't have to..." His voice quivered. "They showed up at my house right before I got the call from you, Officer Lawrence."

"The night of Ryan's murder?" I asked.

Bart nodded, and I prayed his eyeballs wouldn't pop out of his head. "I'm sorry I didn't say anything. I couldn't. I can't. I don't know if they'll attack me now. They showed me all kinds of weapons. A handgun, a knife, a club, a baseball bat, a wooden stake, an axe. I was scared out of my wits. Still am."

Now that was the truth. My nose finally had a moment of relief when he stopped lying, but poor Bart was still terrified.

"Weapons?" I echoed, looking at Sett.

"The variety of them could be to throw us off the real weapon."

"Or they could be a hunter."

"Either way," he said. "Now we know this death wasn't a vampire bite." Turning back to Bart, he dipped his chin. "So what was the real cause of death?"

Bart smiled grimly. "Good old fashioned lights out." He gestured with both hands raised over his head. Mimicking the act of holding something, he brought the invisible thing down as if whacking the victim's head. "Ryan was hit."

"With the VCR," I said.

"That's right. At least, that's what his blood smeared across the VCR suggests," he said with a nod.

Sett stuck out his hand over the steel table. Bart looked at it like it was a snake at first, almost jumping back away from Sett's offer, but after a moment, he took Sett's hand, and they shared a firm handshake.

"Thank you," Sett said. "I'm going to tell you the same thing I told Noema. You should not be alone. If that means you need to come stay at the station or at my house, then that's what we'll do until we catch this killer."

Bart visibly relaxed. "Let me clean up here, and I'll bring a novel to the station."

"Can I ask something?" I started. "What was the bite created with? Or was it just a coincidence that a bat had gotten to him right before he died?"

"It wasn't a bite," he said. "I'm sorry, I've been so nervous my brain isn't working right. I should be giving you all these details now."

Sett pulled a notepad from inside his coat pocket. From the other side of the coat, he took out a pen that he popped between his lips while he reached for a third item. Those pockets were like Mary Poppins's purse. He produced a digital camera that he used to take a snapshot of Ryan's neck before tucking it back into his coat to free up his hands for writing notes.

"The killer used makeup to create the look," Bart continued. "The holes seemed to be punched in with very small, thin scissors, which I only realized because the holes are smaller the deeper they go and wide at the opening. There's an uneven prick on the inside too."

"Stage makeup?" I asked, as I tried to recall if any of the construction crew members had had access to the attic in Everland Theater where we stored costumes and stage makeup.

"I'm not sure," he said. "I traced the brand to something called Siren's Style." Siren? Was that the brand Chanel wore? She was the only siren I knew, but that didn't mean she wore the makeup named after her special abilities. "Whatever it is," he continued, "it's expensive. I did a little research to see if I could figure out who this person was."

Expensive makeup and small scissors. That sounded a lot like two things Chanel would have. Plus, Ryan had rejected her —in front of me and Hattie.

What better place to off him and leave him for dead than in the spot where he rejected her? Or the worst place, if you considered how clearly it gave her away...

I turned this over in my mind as we shuffled outside the lab. I was grateful for the fresh air while we waited for Bart to clean up. Though his fear faded a little after Sett offered protection, even a dash of odor in that small room was too much for me.

Once the door clicked shut, I turned to Sett. "I think you need to interview Chanel next."

Sett's stony brow twisted. "Chanel?"

"The sewing scissors and the makeup? I think it's her brand."

"What would be her motive?"

"She hit on Ryan twice, and he rejected her. Twice."

Sett sucked air through his teeth. Nobody rejected Chanel. She was gorgeous, perfect, and if she really wanted to snag them, she could charm them with her siren song. Her singing only worked on those who weren't interested in someone else, though. Had she tried singing for Ryan and his love for his girl-friend only dug the knife of rejection deeper into Chanel's ego?

I shook my head. "But the collection of weapons doesn't make sense."

"Actually," he said. "It does. Her late husband was a big game hunter from Alaska before she turned him away from that lifestyle and made him go vegan."

I stared up at him. "Really? I didn't know that."

"You're friends with Mae and you didn't know that? I guess the old gal really can keep a secret or two."

"Or Chanel threatened her."

Sett laughed. "Mae doesn't respond to threats."

"True. So you think Chanel still has her husband's hunting weapons?"

He folded his arms and met my gaze. "I think I'm confused about why Rufus attacked you and ran off if he's not our suspect. Any chance she knew him and tried to frame him? It makes me wonder if she threatened him too."

"He's not exactly a handsome man. I can't imagine Chanel chatting him up."

"That's a good point. But in my research about Rufus, I found he doesn't always have the best practices with his films.

He goes to exotic locations and has been accused of leaving the area trashed when he's done using it as a set. Whatever he can do to get a good film for low cost."

"Okay, yeah, that'd piss her off." My hand shot to my mouth as a thought overtook me. "Wait! Chanel mentioned something about an environmental lawsuit with Ryan's company. I didn't think anything of it because he said the case was closed and I smelled the truth. But maybe it still upset Chanel?"

"If she was hitting on Ryan to try to change him the way she did with her late husband, she'd be following a pattern."

"I guess rehabilitating them by marrying them is better than killing them."

Sett grimaced. "But it didn't work this time."

"Because Ryan was in love with someone else."

"So she could have..."

I nodded. "Yep."

As we both considered this, my stomach broke the short silence with a groan. Without a word, Sett produced a home-made granola bar from a pocket inside his coat and offered it to me. Those Mary Poppins pockets were really rather quaint and cozy for such a stoic man.

I took the treat, unwrapping the parchment paper and sinking my teeth into the delicious combination of granola, butter, and honey. Sett sweetened the bar using his own recipe of maple syrup and with peanut butter chips mixed in, leaving it free of chocolate chips.

Even though we were discussing murder and the potential killer could be a friend of ours, calm settled in my bones.

This was one thing that would never change—Sett's home-made food was to die for.

CHAPTER 14
A CRIME OF FASHION

BEFORE TALKING WITH CHANEL, Sett insisted we gather every possible detail. Two hours after our visit with Bart, we found ourselves buried in work at the station. Sett wanted to go into a chat with her armed to the fangs with as much information as we could find. That way, we'd be able to pull out the loose threads in her story.

I'd had to bite my tongue when I wanted to suggest that my nose could do the job for us. Of course, it didn't always detect the emotions of a skillful liar. And if the murderer felt little to no guilt? I couldn't smell that either. Facts and information would always be more reliable investigative tools.

Poring over the details of the lawsuit against Level Head Construction Company left me hungry enough to ask for another round of snacks from Sett's Mary Poppins pockets. It didn't help that I'd skipped dinner to join him while Hattie and Bette took the kids to Roller Shakes for burgers and fries. Bart had opted to go out for a burger too, which Sett approved as long as Bart promised to stay in a public place.

My mouth watered at the thought of a juicy cheeseburger with extra cheese. Sett's homemade beef jerky rivaled a cheeseburger's flavor, but I wanted something warm in my stomach. Too bad murder investigations didn't wait for food to cook. And as Sett said before, two heads were better than one.

So here I was, investigating and starving along with Sett.

I speed-read through newspapers to find out what the public knew about the lawsuit—what Chanel likely learned about it—while Sett got more of the insider details by making a few calls.

Ripping off a piece of the jerky with my teeth, I savored the hint of BBQ and unfolded another newspaper.

Ever since Sett discovered a picture of me in the newspaper, he'd started a collection. The storage room at the back of the station was piled waist-high with old and recent newspapers from Bewitcher's Beach to Shadowvale University, and all the way to Hollywood.

He'd said that someday, maybe, we'd spot a news story about the Titan family. If my family's prophecies and magic were as famous as the witches at Shadowvale had once suggested, they'd appear in the papers again one day.

I sighed and flipped the large, inky paper to the next page. This newspaper was dated two days after Chanel's husband had passed away. I reread the obituary.

"Survived by his wife and two young sons. He cared for the environment and enjoyed adding odds and ends to his unusual collections."

I snorted. Unusual? How about *scary?* Chanel may have turned him into a vegan, but if he kept his hunting gear around, maybe she didn't make him into the man she'd hoped.

The obituary produced nothing helpful other than a quote from Chanel. "He was loved by everyone here in Bewitcher's Beach as well as by his friends back in Alaska." This suggested he could have kept in touch with old hunting buddies. Maybe Chanel, herself, maintained a friendship with them, which meant she had an extra access port to people who collected an assortment of weapons.

Sett hung up the phone and swiveled his office chair to face me. "Level Headed Construction Company lost the lawsuit. But it was determined that Ryan was not involved personally, and he fired the workers who did the dumping."

"Do you think Chanel found that out?"

He pursed his lips and blew out a slow breath through his nose. "It depends on how carefully she researched this. She may have heard about it when the crew came to work on Everland Theater and her...passion...fired her up enough not to care."

"Is it time to talk with her yet?" I offered him an eager smile, like a kid asking for candy in Triton's Taffy shop.

He shook his head. "I keep thinking you're more patient than you used to be, but then I realize you've just gotten better at hiding it."

I laughed. "That's not true. I waited three days for you to look into Bart, and I didn't bother you once!"

"Does three voice messages left on my answering machine at home and on my cell phone not count as bothering me?"

I narrowed my eyes as if giving this careful thought. "That depends on what you consider annoying."

"People who roll their cars through stop signs," he said, lifting a finger. He counted off the rest of his list one-by-one. "People who leave their junk on the beach—I gotta give that one to Chanel, nature is not a trash can."

"So basically all people who break the law?"

He ignored me and continued counting. "People like me who overstep and shove their nose where it doesn't belong." He had me pinned with his gaze as he held up the three fingers that kept track of his annoyances. "We haven't talked about my behavior. I crossed a line with Crow. I shouldn't have harassed him."

A blush crept over my neck. Forget red rings on my throat, my whole neck was red, but not because Sett sounded apologetic. His pushiness over Crow was in the past, and I just didn't have the capacity to revisit the past yet. If I thought too much about the way things were, I'd have to face the changes that'd happened since. Sure, I was okay with the breakup, but I'd become comfortable with the life I had, the Bewitcher's Beach I knew, only to end up haunted by a prophecy that was both from my past and part of my supposed future. I'd wanted to know my missing family for as long as I could remember, but in that time, I'd created a family here in town. What if, like the prophecy, they wanted to change that?

"We don't need to talk about it." We did, but that didn't mean I wanted to.

"We do," he insisted. Sett was as stubborn as his rock-hard exterior suggested. "Like I said, I crossed the line. I want to call it protective because I didn't like how Crow's absence made you feel, but it wasn't my place. I have to remind myself that my job is protecting the citizens of this town from danger, and that's where the line is drawn. I'm sorry for butting in."

I forced an agreeable smile, though something about his apology didn't feel right. Everything he said was true, but facts and feelings didn't always align. I knew, logically, that he'd been too pushy, but I didn't hate it. I'd only avoided him because it was the right thing to do, not because I wanted it, or because I wanted him to stop caring...

"It's okay."

"It's not."

"Okay, it's not. But I mean, it's okay now. You apologized, and it's in the past."

"From now on, you tell me when you want any...help. Agreed?"

I nodded. But what if I liked that pushy, aggressive side of Sett when it came to protecting me?

The chair squeaked as he pushed it away from the desk and stood. "Okay, Speedy. Let's go talk to Chanel."

"Speedy?" I said, following in his wake. "Speedy? Really? I don't speed." That was a lie, but he'd never caught me driving too fast through Bewitcher's Beach. Yet.

He waved me out of the station and turned around to lock the door as he spoke. "There're two more things that annoy me: speeders and impatience."

"So I annoy you?" I asked as we followed the sidewalk past the clinic.

"Well you certainly don't bore me."

I shot him a death glare, but he only cracked a corner smile.

That smile faded when we stepped up to Chanel's boutique and Sett's expression became business-like.

Inside the shop, I enjoyed the floral scent of perfume, which I much preferred over the coroner's lab.

Chanel paused her task of hanging chemise nightgowns on black wire hangers. She turned and greeted us with the same flirtatious grin she gave everyone. She had a way of making you feel important, seen, but also putting you in your place, like a single look from her reminded you that you'd never be as striking as her. Not that I cared. I'd go mad with the amount of attention Chanel drew. But it was an interesting feeling to have your confidence boosted by her simple smile while simultaneously dashing it on the rocks.

Another smell seeped into the cloud of hibiscus perfume.

Oh no...The knots in my gut tightened as ammonia soured the air—again. Chanel could flash us a smile all she wanted, but the stench of her sudden nerves didn't lie.

"We'd like to ask you a few questions," Sett said.

"About?" She blinked innocently, her thick lashes flashing rapidly at Sett. It did nothing to soften his emotionless expression.

He remained blank as he dove into the usual interview. "I understand that you had a brief relationship with Ryan."

"Relationship?" Her painted lips dropped open and she narrowed her eyes at me. "Did you tell him this?"

"Relationship is the wrong word," he said.

"He's not great with words," I jumped in.

Sett made an odd noise as he double-glanced at me and then returned his attention to Chanel. "I've talked to almost everyone who was around Ryan the day he died, but I didn't know you'd spoken with him that day too. Is it true that you showed interest in him and he...denied you?" I must have rubbed off on Sett because he didn't usually dive that deep so quickly.

Chanel showed sudden interest in the gown on the rack in front of her. Running it between her fingers, she sighed. "Yes." Lavender filled the air. This was true, but of course, I already knew that. The odd thing was, the smell of her truthful answer didn't come with the odor of regret or annoyance or anything that would suggest Ryan's rejection made her mad.

But she *was* mad that day. I remembered the smoke. Maybe it wasn't about the rejection though. She'd also been angry when she slipped a snide comment to him about the lawsuit.

"Did you know much about Ryan's company?" I asked.

She arched a penciled eyebrow. After a long pause, she said, "I did. I check to make sure everybody doing business in Bewitcher's Beach keeps our shores clean."

This was nothing but the truth, and once she said it, Chanel didn't seem to hesitate. Her voice was as clear as it was firm.

"And when you found out Level Head wasn't environmentally conscious, did that make you mad?" Sett asked.

"Of course. This was the first job his company had after the lawsuit closed, and I wasn't pleased that he merely fired two men who dumped the concrete, not the other crew members who were there at the dumping. He should have fired half of his crew, and I was going to convince him of that. But I didn't kill him. Why would I when I had a plan to change his mind?"

The smell on this one was muddy. Lavender still lingered in the air with the scent of her perfume, but her nerves were rising to the surface too. A hint of fishy guilt came with them.

Sett continued. "But your plan was stalled when he turned you down." A huff slipped out of her, but Sett wasn't deterred. "We found the same brand of makeup that you use on the victim's body."

"I use multiple brands," she said, the nerves still building but not enough for me to call her a liar. There was no guilt mixed in, just basic anxious feelings. "It changes with my mood. And a lot of people use the same brands."

"Chanel, did you keep any of the weapons your late husband had collected?"

She scoffed. "I don't want to talk about this anymore."

"Then we can make it quick if you answer one simple question," he said, folding his arms to show that he meant business. "Where were you between ten and eleven pm the night Ryan's body was found at Mockbuster?"

Her tongue darted out, smearing a bit of her perfect lipstick. When her lashes fluttered, she sucked in a breath. "I was here, folding clothes for opening the next day. Like I always do."

"Can anyone corroborate that?"

"Triton," she said, pointing in the direction of the taffy

owner's shop. "He always comes over at closeup to help with anything I need. I'll get him, and you can ask him yourself."

Sett opened his mouth, but Chanel had already shoved past him. Within two minutes, she'd returned with her arm linked through the lanky human from next door.

When Triton assured us he was with her that night during the hours of Ryan's murder, that was that. He smelled one hundred percent truthful. Not a drop of fear or guilt or anything other than pure confidence, happiness, truth, and hope came from Triton. It didn't matter if the whole room had filled with the stench of her guilt, Triton had seen her here.

We left the boutique with sighs on our lips. As much as I didn't want to find out Chanel was a killer, it made the most sense, and now we were back to the first square. She had motive, she wore the makeup used on the body, and she had sewing scissors the exact size of the holes in Ryan's neck—something Bart confirmed when I told him to check the size of seam scissors.

But her alibi was strong enough for now.

"I think we're missing something," I said as we weaved through a stream of people walking through town. Night had beckoned a full-moon that brightened the center park. The shop's overhangs kept us in the dark, but I still felt someone watching us in the shadows.

The hair on the back of my neck prickled, and I followed the feeling with my eyes. I looked up to a light pole where the sensation was the strongest. Nothing was there. Not a camera, not someone in a window.

But after a moment, a shadow flickered in the dim sky. Two leathery wings blended with the blue-black, and when I blinked, the bat vanished into the night.

"I agree," Sett said, too lost in thought to notice the bat or that I recoiled from it.

"You're sure Rufus left town?" I asked.

He looked at me now, gray eyes searching my face. "No, but the executive producer of his next film finally returned my call earlier this evening." I tilted my head at him. I'd sat right across from him while he was on the phone, but I'd been too engrossed in the newspapers to hear his conversations. "She said Rufus was on the phone that night. They were discussing business about a new film."

"I thought he was on a date with his wife?"

"Didn't you say his wife was mad at him? I'm willing to bet that was why."

"So Chanel is our only suspect." And who the heck was the bat that kept watching—and biting—me? Chanel's makeup couldn't shift her shape. She may have had enchanted thread, but I'd never heard of magic makeup. In fact, I knew magic makeup wasn't real because Bette desperately wanted to wear makeup, and as a ghost, it was impossible. She'd even tried asking witches to create something for her.

"Chanel *was* our only suspect. Now she has a solid alibi," he confirmed.

My mouth popped open as a thought struck me. "What if she didn't have an alibi for a second murder?"

But Sett didn't hear me.

Two teenagers darted behind Roller Shakes with paper bags shaped like bottles in their hands. Sett was already on their tails before I even caught the stinging, warm smell of tequila from their bags. He didn't even see the two women jaywalking from the rink's parking lot to the field across the street.

A strike of nerves spiked my pulse. Bewitcher's Beach was becoming a petty crime hotspot, and I was hating the changes more and more every day.

CHAPTER 15
ALONE

I MULLED over my idea for two days. In the spare moments between running a jam-packed shop and sneaking quality time with my kids, I considered baiting the killer.

Yes, baiting her. Or him.

And Hattie was on board.

I yanked the chain to the neon sign in Mockbuster's window. The light announcing that the store was open went dark. A couple walked up to the door right as I locked it. Through the glass, I caught their muffled curses, and I wasn't spared from their death glares.

I ripped my gaze away, not allowing them to guilt me. I'd hardly had time to breathe, much less eat, and the store was a wreck. Trash tumbled out of the little can next to the register, shelves were picked clean, the mini fridge needed to be restocked with sodas, and the return stacks would grow as tall as me soon if I didn't replenish the shelves.

Blowing out a breath, I marched to the trash and yanked the plastic bag out. Twisting the top, I carried it to the back door. I shoved through the door into the little alley behind Mockbuster where I kept my van and a dumpster.

I gave the bag a swing and launched it over the edge of the dumpster. It fell inside with the clang of aluminum from all my empty cans of soda.

Before I turned back to the door, a shadow flickered from beneath the other side of the van. My wolf ears perked, and I caught the sound of footsteps. My heart rate doubled when leathery wings expanded and shot out from behind the van. It duck and dove, so I spun around and jogged toward the door.

I could have sworn I heard the pounding of feet between the slap of wings flapping, but I didn't stick around to risk another bite. I grabbed the doorknob and twisted, shoving the weight of my entire body into the door. Bursting inside Mockbuster, I slammed the door shut and pressed my back against it.

My breath came in short gasps. I hardly had time to breathe before facing another death glare. Ghost stares were far more threatening than an angry look from a human or a witch or a gargoyle, though I'd take a scary look over another bat bite any day.

Hattie folded her arms. "You didn't tell me you planned to close up early. Are you okay?"

"The bat came at me again. And this isn't early or closing. These are my usual hours."

"Early for this new rush," she said. "It's only seven forty-five. You've been staying open way past the kids' bedtimes on the weekends."

"Yeah, and I'm sick of it. I barely have time to see my own children, and the noise of customers has been keeping Jovi awake." Though Jovi didn't mind. He used the excuse to read and reread a new book he'd somehow snagged a copy of that wasn't supposed to release for another month. *Harry Potter and the Sorcerer's Stone* had consumed his attention. He'd become as obsessive with this witch and wizard story as I was about solving this murder—and the mysterious bat.

The little beast continued to pop up several times a day, chittering outside Mockbuster's windows and then flitting away before I could talk to it. It followed me whenever I drove the carpool to summer camp or swung by the school to pick them up after it ended. But no matter what, the bat kept its distance, which only gave me a little comfort.

And the more I thought about when the snappy critter bit me, the more I was convinced it was setting up for Ryan's murder.

"The point is—" Hattie's voice sliced through my thoughts. "You're not supposed to be alone until the killer is behind bars."

I waved her off and marched to the shop's computer. At my feet, stacks of returned tapes reached to my waist. The shelves were bare, and I ended up having to dig through piles to find the requested videos for my customers. There simply weren't enough hours in the day to fulfill every need.

Thank goodness for the night. Like Jovi, I shirked a few hours of sleep to get what I wanted done.

"That's not a thing anymore," I said as I started scanning returns into the computer. "The killer isn't Rufus, nor are they a vampire. That's why the bat isn't part of this investigation anymore."

"But it won't leave you alone, and you said last night that you think the bat and the killer are connected. Vampire or not."

I set the tape down on the desk and slumped into the stool. Rubbing my palms over my face, I released a slow breath. Once I looked at Hattie, I nodded. "I know. But like Sett said, we can't prove anything with the bat unless we can communicate with it. It's suspicious because of the timeline of the bat's attack. The bat bit me, which forced me to leave the shop empty, where Ryan was killed with no witnesses."

"So the bat is a magical companion of some sort?"

"Possibly."

I knew anybody—witch or not—could create a special bond with an animal harboring magic. But it was wildly rare. At Shadowvale University, I'd realized Stevie had this rare ability. She could always communicate with animals easily. She'd even taught me a trick or two about speaking with animals.

"So the bat is basically an accomplice," Hattie said with a whistle. "That's a doozy of a twist. But an easy answer to our problems: catch the bat and tell Stevie to have a chat with it. Then we'll have our killer's name."

I rolled my eyes. "Don't you think I tried that? That bat is impossible. I can't get within ten feet of it. It's always just flying around, watching." I shivered. "And any time I've asked for someone else's help catching it, the bat somehow knows. It disappears for hours, only showing up when I'm—" I stopped and stole a side-glance.

"Alone?" she finished for me, tutting her tongue against the roof of her mouth.

"Anyway." I pushed past her judgmental sounds. "I'm not letting Stevie anywhere near that bat unless it's trapped in a cage. These bites will leave a scar." I lifted my arm to show her the marks of the beast's tiny fangs.

Hattie peered at the scar and whistled again. "So, what's your plan?"

Sliding my gaze to her, I folded my arms. "How do you know I have a plan?"

"Because you're my best friend and you're Noema Detective Titan."

"I'm Noema *Wolf*." I insisted. She let out a little huff, and my eyes narrowed. "What?"

"I know half the reason you're throwing yourself into this investigation is to avoid thinking about that prophecy."

My mouth dropped open, but a sudden well of emotion

lodged in my throat. I couldn't speak. Arguing was useless anyway. Hattie was right, and I hadn't even realized it.

The bat bothered me, sure, but the prophecy bothered me more. I'd *left* Crow. My only relationship with a reaper was done, over, capiche. Deep down, I hated what that suggested— that I wasn't really a Titan woman. That the prophecy wasn't talking about my family. That the witches at Shadowvale and I had made some kind of mistake when we followed the threads that tied me to The Book of Prophecies and the Titan family.

My voice came out small, and I toyed with the keyboard, tracing my index finger over the "escape" button. "What if it was all a dream that I woke up from when Crow and I broke up?" Or a nightmare, depending on what it meant to be part of this mysterious witch family.

Hattie didn't need more context. She reached an icy hand across the counter and cooled my werewolf fever. The chill of her fingers soothed my skin where they hovered over the scar.

"Oh, Noema, darling. You know that's not true. You have a family somewhere, and you're halfway to finding them."

I forced myself to meet her gaze, but she was a swimming blur behind the tears welling in my eyes. "That's the problem. I've been so focused on finding them, I didn't stop to think about how knowing them might change my entire life. It already has. The prophecy saying I must marry a reaper is really just too much..." Worry twisted my voice until my breath faded.

What would my life look like as a Titan woman? What would it look like if I never found my family?

I loved the home I'd made here in Bewitcher's Beach. I didn't need more, but I still longed for answers. Why had they abandoned me? The fact that they never came looking for me dug that thought in deeper.

I'd spent these past few weeks blaming the crowds for my

fear of change, but it was always rooted in my past. Maybe I needed therapy.

Blinking back tears, my gaze shifted to the windows where blue-gray moonlight filtered in. A good run on the beach during the full moon would do, but I wasn't ready to be alone, and Sett only ran on the job. Hattie would rather die again than run, and I didn't think running with my children was safe for any of us.

I sucked in a shuddering breath. The tears cleared from my eyes, and I lifted my chin. "So about my plan."

"About your plan," she repeated, giving me a firm nod to signal that she was ready for the subject change.

"We bait the killer." She whistled a high and sharp sound that forced me to fold my wolf ears back. When she finished, I dove into the explanation. "If Chanel or someone else was upset about Level Head's lawsuit and came after Ryan for continuing to operate his company, then they'll be just as mad if a new manager comes in and continues working with the remaining guilty crew members."

"What new manager?"

"You're looking at her." I popped a thumb in my direction. "Meet Level Head's head of crew. We're going to say that one of the guilty crew members got promoted. I did my research. There's a guy named Teddy at Level Head who was working the day of the concrete dumping. He's a witness, and about the same height as me. He's also got so much facial hair, you can barely see his face."

She smirked. "I've seen him. Bette and I nicknamed him Hairy."

"Well, meet the new Hairy Teddy."

Channeling Chanel, she arched a brow. "You hate acting."

"I hate killers more."

"You hate not having answers."

"That too." And could she blame me? I'd spent my entire

adult life wondering about the other half of a life I couldn't remember. I craved to fill in the blanks. Scanning more tapes into the computer, I continued. "Here's the thing. I smelled fear and a little guilt on Chanel. Also—and Sett won't acknowledge this as a change to her alibi—but she can manipulate men who like her. Triton has always had eyes for Chanel."

Hattie solidified her hands enough to help me with the rentals. When I scanned a tape, she took it and surged toward the spot on the shelf where it belonged. Returning to retrieve the next tape, she asked, "Wouldn't you still smell guilt if Triton was lying?"

"Not necessarily. If he's flooded with good feelings about Chanel, it may have masked any negative feelings."

"Well, you've convinced me!" Hattie threw up her hands. "I'll get the costume, you figure out how to get the news to Chanel."

"Already done. If Sett approves, I'm going to give Mae the green light to gossip at Chanel's boutique. Once the gossip spreads, I'll have Mae drop information about the specific day and time that Teddy will be walking the theater to approve changes and resume construction. If Chanel is angry enough about the lawsuit, she'll show up to whack him. And if the killer isn't Chanel, Mae will have spread the word around town for everyone else to hear. Whoever wasn't satisfied with how Level Head handled the dumping of toxic waste is about to be exposed."

"That's a solid plan," she said. "As long as you don't actually get whacked." Using her halfway solid hand, she knocked it against the desktop.

"That's what Sett will be here for."

"I shouldn't have doubted. Sett wouldn't approve if you weren't one hundred million percent protected."

Once we finished returning the rentals to their rightful

locations, Hattie disappeared into Everland Theater, but only on the condition that I stayed on the phone with Sett while she was gone.

His approval came quicker and easier than I expected. Poor Sett was so underwater with all of the crime bearing down on Bewitcher's Beach that he actually agreed to let me bait a murderer.

The puff of his sigh came through the other line. He blew air right into the receiver, and I had to pull the phone away from my ear until he spoke again. "I'm insane for agreeing to this, but closing this case will keep people safe. I can't be everywhere at once. Investigating falls to the wayside when I'm running around stopping a hundred other crimes."

"You need a night off," I said.

"If I ever get a free second, I'll bring shepherd's pie over, and we can watch *Mulan*. Stevie told me I've been missing the greatest movie of all time."

I laughed. "She says that about every new Disney movie."

"But this one has a talking dragon and a cricket, apparently."

Another laugh escaped me. "When did you see Stevie?"

"At their summer camp. One of their teachers was mugged when he was out of town for the weekend. I had to squeeze in a moment to grab his statement and forward the information to the cops in that jurisdiction. My only free second was during camp hours, unfortunately. But the kids convinced me to stay and read to them, which I've been missing. I used to have time to volunteer every week at the library."

"Maybe you can get back to it when everything calms down around here."

"I hope those witches finish rebuilding the protection spell soon. I need these tourists to get out of my hair."

Hearing him say this suddenly boosted my spirit. "I've been thinking the same thing!"

"Great minds."

"All these changes are sort of freaking me out," I admitted.

Sett's voice was soft when he said, "This definitely isn't the change I wanted to see either."

When Hattie came back with a makeshift construction costume, a convincingly realistic beard, and a hard hat for me to wear tomorrow night, I bid Sett goodbye.

I was never alone lately, but it felt really good not to be alone in my feelings either. Neither of us enjoyed the changes in Bewitcher's Beach, but talking about it together helped ease my fears.

CHAPTER 16
BAITED

AFTER A WEEK of laying the gossip groundwork, summer melted into fall. Falling leaves and cooler weather always came early in Bewitcher's Beach. By the first of August, we welcomed orange and brown trees and the crisp crunch of their leaves beneath our feet.

Though tourists still swarmed the town, the threat of rain and clouds drove them away from the beach. They lingered, maybe waiting for the fall festival coming in only a few weeks. Gloomier weather kept people from window shopping and long walks too. Unfortunately, this pushed tourists inside where they crowded every inch of Roller Shakes and the shops.

Without much to do, more customers piled into Mockbuster, cramming each corner with bodies and wiping out the entire wall of candy. Nearly every video was rented as visitors stole away to their rooms at The Oyster Inn to wait out today's downpour.

Thankfully, most of the renovations for Everland Theater were indoors, so the killer would still believe Teddy planned to arrive back into town tonight to give the project the go-ahead.

The time was set for his walkthrough, which was exactly

the same time as Bewitcher's Beach's annual town meeting to discuss the fall festival. According to both tradition and Mae's gossip, neither Hattie nor I would be able to accompany him to discuss the changes, because we never—never—missed the fall festival meeting.

But of course this time, Hattie and I would be absent, and it was worth it to catch a murderer.

I'd instructed Mae to drop details about how our meeting was to take place early in the evening, and then it was said that Teddy would be bouncing back out of town before he returned again with the entire crew.

This was the killer's only chance to catch him alone.

Now all I had to do was wait until the clock struck 7:45. The town's meeting was set for twenty-five minutes from now, which meant the baiting would begin soon.

Thankfully, the shop was busy enough to keep me occupied until then. When I wasn't scanning rentals and smiling at customers, I was on the phone. It rang incessantly until I finally found a second to answer.

Madam Rowena's voice came through the other line. It'd been months since I last heard from the dean of Shadowvale University, the witch heading the recreation of the protection spell for Bewitcher's Beach, *and* the lead study on *The Book of Prophecies*. One of the last times I spoke with her, she informed me about the marital prophecy for Titan women. She'd explained that the lines in *The Book of Prophecies* said I was fated to marry a reaper. Now she had much better news.

"There's a lead," Madam Rowena said, skipping pleasantries and getting right down to business. "I believe I can trace the Titan family by cross-referencing the creation of certain spells mentioned in *The Book of Prophecies* with notable events in *History of the Modern Witch*."

"Do you—" I swallowed. "Do you think the Titan family is still around?"

"It's possible. Especially since the discovery of animal scrying was only two years ago, and nobody is accredited to its discovery. The prophecy about the Titan women is the only prophecy to mention someone with the language of fauna. These are the cross-references to which I am referring. Do you understand, Noema?"

I wasn't a witch exactly, so I knew why Madam Rowena was questioning me, but I didn't love how it sounded. I understood perfectly. "Of course," I said.

"No," she blew a breath into the receiver. "I'm saying, do you understand what this means? If we locate the Titan witches, everything could change. Everything." I bristled, every muscle in my body going taut at the word. *Everything changing*. "We're nearing completion on the protection spell as well. There are three more elements we've been unable to identify. Once we pin those down—which we think will be soon, within days, even—the best witches at Shadowvale will be coming to Bewitcher's Beach to cast it, and then I can really throw myself into studying *The Book of Prophecies*. That will speed up the discovery of the Titan witches."

"What if..." My voice faltered. "What if they're not alive?"

Madam Rowena wasn't great at speaking softly. She simply huffed and gave me the cold-hard facts. "That would be disappointing, but even finding more of their work, where they lived, any information on them, can inform our magic. The better we understand magic, the more we can design life-changing spells like the protection spell, powerful healing, and seal our bonds with familiars and magical animals." Her voice became muffled for a moment before she returned to the phone. "I haven't got another second to spare. Take care, Noema."

With that, the line went dead. I didn't even have a chance

to say goodbye, but it was just as well because the clock had ticked past 7:40 and I was running late to the bait.

I slammed the phone on the receiver and hurried the last customers out the door. Locking up, I bolted next door to climb into my costume and rehash the plan with Hattie.

She floated alongside me as we paced through the empty aisles of Everland Theater. White plastic tarps covered the cherry red seats, adding to the haunted air of the empty building.

The theater that was once full of life and movement was laid bare. Actors, audience, and stage crew had abandoned it when transformation shut it down and construction tape wrapped around the outside. The yellow and black warning signs were crisscrossed in front of the double doors that were usually swung open wide and welcoming the cast and crew for rehearsals at this time of year.

I draped my fingers over the plastic, letting a breath escape me.

On the eve of fall, Everland Theater followed the changes of the season, looking darker and more hollow than ever before. I usually loved the autumn weather. Beckoning chillier temperatures kept my wolf fever cool, but this year, I'd grown used to the heat. Fall brought a new school year for the kids, new teachers, and new demands. New releases at Mockbuster would pile in with holidays on the horizon. Everything was new, new, new, and I wanted the old.

My old life, before I knew about the prophecy and that I was related to the Titan witches, was simpler. Now I had a name for my family, but the name led nowhere beyond the marriage prophecy. That I knew of.

Did I want to know more? This prophecy had already pressured me to stay with Crow longer than I should have. I led him on, complained about him, and caused a competitive rift between him and Sett all because I wanted to do right by the family I'd never met.

Would knowing more only drop heavier pressure on my shoulders? I was only one woman, one werewolf, a single mother raising four kids on my own. I couldn't carry the weight of change.

I'm Noema Wolf. Not Noema Titan.

And yet, even thinking this caused my stomach to tighten. For so long, I'd wanted to meet the family I couldn't remember. Could I really allow this fear to keep me from them?

Hattie surged her non-corporeal form into the seat I was touching. Her bottom half disappeared into the white tarp as she tilted her head at me. "Are you worried this is too dangerous?"

"The bait?" I shook my head. "No. Sett will be here any second."

"Okay, but even under all that fake beard, I can see the ocean in your eyes, Noema."

I quickly swiped a finger at the corner of my eye, catching a teardrop. I hadn't even realized my thoughts were leaking out of me. Pushing out a breath, I stood a little taller. Hairy Teddy beat my height by a couple inches anyway, and I needed to resemble him as much as possible to pull a confession out of the killer.

"I'm just not ready for everything to change."

"Nobody is ever ready for change, doll." Her voice was actually gentle, which was a feat for Hattie. "We get comfortable with our lives. But comfort isn't always good either. You were comfortable with half-finished screenplays, but you wanted a complete story. Heck, everybody in Bewitcher's Beach was comfortable with their lives when the protection spell was still standing, but the second it fell, somebody was killed. Now look at this town. We've had a string of murders a mile long because nobody was prepared for any crime, much less the worst crime of them all. We were too comfortable with the routine of it all."

"Yeah but losing the protection spell was a terrible change."

"Was it? Losing it helped us discover that it was real. It was once a belief, but now we have the proof of it in *The Book of Prophecies*. Now we have the brightest and most brilliant witches at Shadowvale working to recreate it which could lead to protection spells beyond Bewitcher's Beach."

I nodded half-heartedly, thinking back to Rowena's words about how they could expand the magic to protect people in other areas. All murders and assaults could essentially end as the magic made it impossible to attack someone. Police could catch assailants in the attempt, and nobody would get hurt. With *The Book of Prophecies*, the witches could do great things.

"In order to have more, we have to deal with a little change," she said.

More what? More rules and demands on my life? Like marrying a reaper when all I really wanted was a family man— or rather, the man my family loved? Stevie had been begging Sett to come over and watch *Mulan* with her.

A door at the back of the theater clicked shut. My wolf ears perked, catching the faint sound of footsteps across the carpeted floor along the back hallway.

"Sett?" I breathed. He was supposed to come in through the side entrance from Mockbuster, not the back door.

Hair stood on end across my arms, and my gaze slid to Hattie.

She nodded, seemingly understanding my line of thought. This was the killer. They were here, and Sett wasn't.

"We can back out," she whispered. That was easy for her to say. I was fast, but I couldn't move like a ghost.

"Too late," I mumbled.

A shadow stretched across the carpet, extending from the hallway and into the carpet on the floor of the theater. Goosebumps prickled over my neck and shoulders. I glanced at the watch on my wrist. Where was Sett? He was slow-moving but never late to an agreed-upon time. He was supposed to be hiding behind the curtains that still framed the spot where the stage once stood, armed and ready to take down the killer after their confession—or threat.

The length of seats distanced me from the hallway. From here, the killer wouldn't be able to see the details of my face. I slipped the hard hat over my ears, covering my curls I'd tied up and tucked away.

Hattie brushed past me in an icy breeze, leaving the whisper of her plan. "I'll get ready to swoop in."

She surged away, vanishing in a blink as the killer stepped out of the hallway.

The shadow approached carefully but quickly and suddenly. When the woman emerged, I saw her familiar face.

Chanel didn't wear a mask or lady's hose over her face like she did when she confronted Bart. Instead, her face full of makeup was in plain sight. Her thick lashes, heavy lipstick, and swooping blonde curls made for the look of a model, not a killer.

Her arms were stiff at her sides, but a black steel object flashed in her grip as she met my gaze. In her other hand, her fingers wrapped around a long silver pole, just like the metal poles used in a rolling clothes rack.

Breath stalled in my throat.

She'd come armed with two weapons.

CHAPTER 17
SIREN'S SONG

"TEDDY," she said, her voice so unlike Chanel. Instead of confident and swanky, the word came out in quiver. She didn't want to do this, but she was angry enough at Level Head to show up here again. I caught the scent of smoke mingled with her fear. "I'm going to need you to shut down this project, then take your company and leave. Is that—is that understood?"

With that, she raised the weapon, the barrel pointing at me from across the row of seats. With one foot snaking in front of the other like she was walking a runway, Chanel inched toward me. Humming a strange tune, she fixed her eyes on me.

The sound caught in the acoustic panels, carrying throughout the theater. When the song—almost like a haunting nursery rhyme—surrounded me, my muscles tensed.

It wasn't magic locking me up, though; it was pure fear, a feeling I hadn't known in a long time. Even though I suspected Chanel, seeing her carrying two weapons proved more shocking than I suspected.

And she was trying to manipulate me with the song—or rather, manipulate Teddy. She likely hoped he wasn't in love, because a siren's song only worked on those seeking attraction to and from others.

She was once a friend. Her sons went to school with my kids, and yet, she was a cold-blooded killer. None of the other murders were like this. Once I uncovered the killers, their heartless ways actually made sense. But I couldn't make sense of this mother, this friend, this woman who just wanted to protect the environment, as someone so violent.

"Chanel, I'm not—"

She reacted by cocking the gun and extending her arm, but it wasn't a sure movement—more of a twitch, a flicker that showed she was wound tight and ready to snap.

I swallowed hard, burying my confession until I felt it was safe to tell her I wasn't really Teddy.

According to the plan, I was supposed to back up slowly, guiding her to where Sett stood so that he could step out and apprehend her. But he wasn't there, and Hattie had vanished, as planned. She was the backup help. In case Sett wasn't able to get to the killer in time, Hattie could swoop in and at least distract them. If she solidified her ghostly body enough, she could even make a grab at the weapon, but that could prove dangerous if Chanel was trigger-happy.

My eyes darted around the theater. Hattie was nearby, I knew it, but she must have heard the quiver in Chanel's voice too. It was dangerous to approach a nervous killer, and Hattie wouldn't put me at risk like that, not without Sett nearby to immediately apprehend Chanel.

"We can make a deal, okay?" She said it in a sing-song voice, though it wasn't uplifting. This song was one of sadness. Without dropping the gun, she raised the metal pole in her other hand. "It will hurt. I won't lie."

"It's me—"

"Shut up! You say another word, and I'll shoot." She'd

shouted out only for her voice to drop to a sudden whisper now. "One hard swing. Just one hard swing. You're supernatural, you're strong."

I frowned and tried to back up, but I was afraid any movement would frighten her. Despite the weapons being trained on me, she was the one pouring out the odor of ammonia. Every sniff was laced with the reminder of her rage. Maybe she was afraid to kill, but that bit of anger was enough to push, push, push her over the edge.

The gun was set and ready, her manicured finger perfectly aligned with the trigger.

Sett, where is my backup?

Chanel formed her red lips around another threat. "If you run, I will have to shoot you. But if you let me knock the memory out of you, I will spare your life."

Knock what memory out of me? Or rather, out of Teddy. Teddy had been on the crew here, but according to his interview with Sett, he hadn't gotten to know anyone in Bewitcher's Beach. He didn't even know Chanel's name.

She raised the bar higher, the stench of rotten guilt sloughing off of her like body odor from her underarms.

I gagged and winced at the same time. The metal pole glinted against the dim light illuminating the theater.

She set her teeth on edge, speaking through them. "I'm sorry it has to be this way."

How had she gotten so close to me? Why didn't I run before the barrel of the gun was inches away? I simply couldn't see the attacker in this friend of mine, even if I smelled it. But she hated to have to do it; that was why she wasn't going to kill me. She only wanted to knock me out. But why?

Why kill Ryan and go so far as to frame a vampire, then show up here only to whack Ryan's replacement?

This wasn't a crime of passionate environmentalism. Her

anger and fear were there, filling the air around her, driving her to step forward and lift the pole above my head, but this was premeditated, planned out, and purposeful in the oddest way.

Did she think she could frame Rufus again?

I couldn't move faster than the bullet, not now that she was so close. And yet, she remained just out of arm's reach. I couldn't grab the gun either.

My fate wasn't to marry a reaper—it was right here, at the whims of Chanel's strange attack.

I could try to drop into my wolf form as she swung, but the movement might trigger her to fire the gun.

In the split second that followed, the pole catching the light at the corner of my eye, I debated back and forth. Should I drop to all fours? Should I take the hit and find myself in the hospital later? What if she hit too hard and I met the same end as Ryan?

I gritted my teeth, readying for impact when a low voice ripped Chanel's attention away from me.

"You don't have to do this, Chanel."

My heart lifted at the sound of Sett's voice, steady, stoic. My backup had finally arrived.

Crystal tears pooled in Chanel's eyes. "You don't understand. It has to be just like the first attack." She adjusted her grip on the pole. "One hard swing."

Ammonia burned and burned in my nose until I had to swallow the contents of my stomach back down my throat.

Sett's footsteps approached from behind me, heavy, firm, and slow. Slow enough not to startle Chanel. Slow enough to keep her calm and listening. Slow was Sett's way. His patience always fascinated me as much as it had irritated me, and he continued to show me how important it was in these high stakes situations.

I still slipped up. Like tonight. I should have waited for Sett to arrive and take his place behind the curtain before I even put on the disguise, but it'd felt like catching the killer was a now-or-never moment.

"I do understand," Sett said. "I'm a protector too, Chanel. You want to protect the environment, and I want to protect the people in it. We're a team, really. But you can't go about it like this." His voice grew louder as he eased closer to us.

Tears slipped down Chanel's cheeks. "I'm so sorry. But I have to. I have to!"

"No!" Sett said, impatience deepening his voice. I slid my gaze to him, my lips falling open. Never had he lost his cool, but the demand with which he barked stalled both Chanel and me in a second of shock.

"Don't make me paralyze you, Sett," she said, desperation and anger and a million other emotions lacing her voice. It left my head spinning and my nose wrinkling.

A lilting hum came from her chest. She heaved a breath and opened her mouth, singing softly, hauntingly.

I broke the rule of Chanel's demand now, shouting out for Sett. "It's her siren song. Cover your ears!"

Chanel ignored me, pitching her voice higher. In seconds, Sett would be frozen, at Chanel's whims, if only for a single moment—but a moment long enough for her to land the blow against my head or shoot me if I tried to run or duck.

The acoustics carried her song as she sang higher and louder.

But Sett didn't stop. He didn't so much as pause from the power of her siren song. When she raised the pole, Sett bolted forward. This was my cue to back up and dodge out of the line of fire.

In shock, Chanel gaped at Sett as he seized her arm and ripped the gun from her hand. Her other arm dropped, and the pole fell with a thump to the carpet at her feet.

Relief flooded me as soon as the weapon was in Sett's grasp

and he spoke. "Chanel, you're under arrest for the attempted assault of Noema Wolf."

"Noema?" Her voice still shook.

My acting and disguise must have been passing, because when she looked at me, confusion rippled from her as the scent of pineapple pizza.

I followed her line of sight when she looked back at Sett. He stepped behind her, casting the shadow of his huge body over her. The darkness swallowed her in shadows, and the clink of his handcuffs followed as he recited her legal rights.

"Of course it didn't work..." Her eyes trailed over me again as I pulled off the hard hat and beard. "Because he loves you."

I nearly swallowed my tongue as I stared back at her. Sett didn't seem to hear her, but my wolf ears caught every suggestion in her words.

Her siren song didn't work on Sett because he only had eyes for me.

CHAPTER 18
CONFESSION

BACK AT BEWITCHER'S Beach police station, I couldn't keep my eyes off of Sett. He sat with his legs spread, his elbows on his knees, and his fingers steepled as he eyed Chanel from across the table. His chair was pushed back, but he was leaning in, listening to every word of her confession.

I'd learned this was a tactic to keep criminals talking. If he busied himself by writing every detail down, she might become nervous about the record he marked in ink and clam up. But with his curious eyes on her, and the gentle look on his face coaxing her to speak up, she spilled everything.

Mascara streamed down her cheeks in black streaks tinged with the blue shimmer of her eyeshadow and turquoise lid liner. Pity wound around my heart at the sight of her tears and blotchy red face.

Her children were at home with a teenage babysitter. I couldn't imagine the phone call she'd have to make to her sisters in the next town over. They'd have to pay both her bail and the babysitter at the same time.

"So," Sett said, straightening and scooting the chair back

toward the table. "I know you're feeling emotional, but when you're ready, I'd like to ask you about Ryan."

She sucked in a shuddering breath. "Ryan refused to replace the entire crew, and I just couldn't abide after what half of them witnessed."

Sett nodded, glancing at me to check if I smelled the truth. This, of course, was true and was confirmed with the soothing smell of lavender.

Chanel calmed more and more as she confessed what had really happened. "Standing by and watching their coworkers dump toxic waste into a protected lake is just as bad as doing the dumping." A hint of her rage trickled in with the calming truth, but neither competed with the all-encompassing fear that strangled her normally-silky voice. "I came to talk with him. To tell him to replace his entire crew, but he argued with me, refusing to listen. I got angrier and angrier."

Did she? Something about the fear in her breath suggested otherwise. Maybe she was just afraid of reliving the murder, and in front of the sheriff. This was it for her; she'd be locked away as a cold-blooded killer. I didn't want to think what that meant for her sweet boys. They'd already lost their elderly father, and now their mother would be ripped away from them too. A twinge twisted between my heart and lungs until I focused on her story. Worry ignited into righteous anger.

Hearing her spell out how she ended the life of an innocent man enraged me for Ryan's girlfriend and the other loved ones in his life. He had a whole marriage ahead of him and a life full of joy. Sure, he shouldn't have been dealing in shady business practices, but he didn't deserve to end up dead on the floor of a video rental shop either.

Chanel sniffed, dabbing at her nose with a tissue before continuing. "He—uh, he grabbed me, so I grabbed the VCR."

"Ryan was hit from behind," Sett said. "When he grabbed you, had he turned around?"

"Yes." Her gaze darted between us. "I waited until he turned away from me so he wouldn't see it coming. I was just so mad."

What of this was true? What wasn't? Chanel's fear overwhelmed everything else again. I was getting really tired of the smell of ammonia.

"So I smacked him as hard as I could with it," she said. "When he fell, I knew it was over. I'd...won. Ryan couldn't continue with the project, and if I were lucky, his whole company would go under after a lawsuit, and the manager's death happened so close together. What company could survive so much bad press? It was my plan."

"But you'd also committed murder," Sett said. "What was your plan to deal with this crime?"

"I framed that vampire who's been visiting town."

"Why specifically him?" I asked.

"I..." Her eyes dropped to the twisted napkin in her hands. She tried to smooth it out, but when her finger touched snot, she let out a little gasp and frowned, bunching it back up in her fist. "I don't know."

This was the pure truth. I noted the floral scent among the burn of ammonia that softened slightly.

"Did you plan any of this with a vampire bat, by any chance?" I asked, desperate to tie up that last loose thread.

Her eyebrows curved, and confusion filled the air around her. "No. I have no idea what you're talking about."

This was another truth, so I dropped any more questions about the bat.

Sett finally pulled out a notepad and scribbled a bit of the confession. "Have you spoken with Bart lately?"

Her head popped up. Shifting her glassy eyes between us,

she finally nodded. "Yeah, I talked to him. I mean, I threatened him to keep the makeup a secret. Otherwise, you would have known it wasn't a vampire."

That was true enough, I supposed.

"And you attempted to kill Ryan's replacement, Teddy?" he asked.

Chanel merely nodded.

I grazed my canine over my bottom lip before my mouth popped open. "You said you wanted me—or him—to forget something. You were going to knock it out of him. What did you mean?"

"Forget the project," she said. Her voice was as flat as the line of her ruby lips.

"But didn't you want him to fire the crew? Shut down the company? Not just forget Everland Theater's construction plans?"

Chanel sighed. "It's complicated. I wanted to...scare him. But I'm not really a killer."

"But you did kill Ryan," Sett said.

After another sigh, Chanel nodded and repeated it back to him. "I did kill Ryan."

She'd done it; we'd caught her. Our bait had worked, and it uncovered a truth that her siren song couldn't manipulate the way she had with Triton.

Finally, this horror was over, though nerves still needled me. Chanel had thrown her whole life down the drain just for a corrupted sense of justice. Her children would be torn from their home and their school and sent away to live with their aunts, all because she was mad at Ryan for arguing.

The tragedy of it twisted me up inside until I could only smell the fresh and earthy scent of rain. I didn't have the energy to mask the air of my own emotions, and at least sadness didn't stink.

While Sett guided Chanel to the holding cell at the back of the station, I shuffled into the front room. I wanted to flop into one of the chairs facing Sett's desk, but I didn't give in to the temptation. I needed to get home and relieve Bette of her babysitting duties. More importantly, I wanted to see my children all safe and snuggled in their beds, even if they were already sound asleep.

There was nothing more peaceful than seeing their little chests rise and fall as they dreamed of kickball and camp, Dunakroo treats and donuts for breakfast.

Exhausted from the draining conversation with Chanel and the high nerve of facing her down at Everland Theater, I dragged myself to the door with the limp of someone who needed a week of sleep. Turning the knob, I yanked it open but didn't rush out into the night alone.

My hackles raised, still thinking of the lingering bat. It was out there, somewhere, ready to swoop in again. Even if it didn't attack me, the constant watching set me on edge. I didn't like that it followed me in the hazy hours of shadows and dim moonlight.

Sett emerged from the holding cell and crossed the length of the station in only a few strides. He'd certainly picked up the pace lately. Gently, he touched my elbow, almost instinctively offering to help keep me upright.

"Are you okay?" he asked.

I almost leaned in to his touch. "I don't know," I answered as honestly as I could. "This is just so sad for Chanel and her family."

"She killed him and then threatened Bart and manipulated Triton, then came to do it again." Swiping a palm over his face, he let out a breath. "But you're right. It is heartbreaking for her family."

I pressed against the door, letting the solid object prop me up. "I mean, I suspected her. It all makes sense, but I think I still expected someone else to show up tonight. She's just a mom and a shop owner and a friend."

More earthy scents filled the room. Sett's own sadness seeped out of him like water running over cracked stone. Shaking his head, he turned his back to me.

"This is the worst part of my job." He spoke as he marched to the desk, where a sealed bag of evidence sat next to neat stacks of paper. Even with all the chaos and crime riddling Bewitcher's Beach, Sett managed to maintain a pristine office. Everything was snug and tight in its place, and the floor was swept. "I hate to see good people make poor choices, and it's even worse when you're the one who has to lock them up."

I couldn't imagine.

Sett opened the bag of evidence and slid out the VCR and then a VHS tape. He quickly met me at the door again. Offering it to me, he said, "But this is the good part of my job. It's not much, but I'll take any piece of good news I can get lately. Crow finally got it out without breaking anything."

I took the tape, turning it over in my hands as if it were a prized diamond or rare artifact. "You talked to Crow?"

He nodded. "He's a good guy. I'm sorry if I crossed a boundary that put a rift between you two."

I shook my head. "It's not that. We're just not right for each other." I ran my thumb along the edge of the video tape. "I'm surprised he came back and worked on getting it out after how frustrating it was to deal with."

Sett slipped his hands into his pockets. "I may have taken it to Roller Shakes and asked for him to try again."

"Sett—"

He held up a hand. "It's okay, he wanted to do something nice for a friend, so he said he was glad I brought it over. He left for another trip today, and I wanted to catch him before he was gone again."

"Did you watch the tape?"

He shook his head. "I didn't get a chance to. I had to meet up with you and Hattie at Everland Theater."

"Yeah, what happened with that? You were late!"

He frowned. "I got a lead on Rufus. His wife returned my calls and said Rufus is coming back into Bewitcher's Beach to turn himself in. I went to the border out by the highway to spot his vehicle and ended up witnessing a car crash. I had to help everyone sort it out before I could leave the scene."

"Is everyone okay?"

"Yes, thankfully. Some young woman was driving her boyfriend home, and they were both under the influence. But it was outside of our borders, so I didn't have to process them. I rushed back into town as fast as I could."

"Rufus is really coming here?"

He shrugged. "That's what his wife said. We'll have to wait and see. Will you be pressing charges for the assault?"

I gingerly touched my neck. "I don't know. I'm too tired to think about anything serious right now."

"I second that."

Lifting the tape, I said, "Thank you for this. I'll let you know if there's anything interesting."

He smiled. "I know you will."

Leaving Sett behind was harder than I expected, but I slipped out into the streets—streets that were finally not too crowded.

I followed the cobblestone sidewalk instead of cutting across the street and through the park for a shortcut. Though there were no cars circling the town now, I didn't like stepping into the street after that close call.

I craned my neck, scanning the sky for any sign of my

stalker. Something small fluttered across the sky, a cutout of black against the gray clouds. I edged closer to the buildings, keeping as far under the overhangs as possible. It was a false sense of security, but enough to ease my mind long enough to observe the shops along the way.

The dog groomers had a sign posted saying they were booked up until the fall festival. Next door, the hair salon had hung a similar announcement. The Oyster Inn's "No" was highlighted on the "No Vacancy" sign. Everybody was booked to the brim, which would bring a boatload of money into Bewitcher's Beach for the fall festival.

Before we knew it, we'd all be swimming in excess money. Last year, I could barely afford to keep the lights on. This was an issue that wouldn't even be on my radar this year.

That was something to be grateful for, changes or not. At least the crowds and noise and speeding cars brought money into town.

Once I made it to Mockbuster, I smiled at the empty aisles. People were enjoying the videos, and even if the lack of options angered a few customers, this was proof of a booming business. I'd have to order more rental copies soon.

Dragging myself up the spiral staircase, I greeted Bette, who informed me that both Dio and Stevie had stayed awake to say goodnight to me. After thanking her, I slipped into the dark bedroom. Two towering bunk beds filled the tight space. It was cozy and full of love—if love was stuffed animals, books, and art supplies.

"Mommy!" Stevie said sleepily. She sat up, a stuffed owl cradled in her arms.

I reached into the top bunk and smoothed her flyaways down. "It's late. I'm surprised you're still awake."

"Tomorrow is Saturday. I can sleep in," she said.

"But you won't."

Dio chimed in from the bed beneath her. "I know I won't. I want to practice my kicks. Soccer season starts in three weeks!"

I ducked to sit at the edge of his bed without hitting my head against the top bunk. "Didn't you practice during camp today?"

He shook his head. "Sports period was canceled."

"I bet Stevie liked that," I said.

Stevie's little voice chimed in from above. "Yeah! Mr. Dylan is gone now. Mrs. B said he's never coming back, and now I'm happy because he was mean and said I couldn't kick or swing hard enough." Her voice pitched higher and louder, threatening to wake Halen and Jovi. I popped up, smacking the crown of my head against the top bunk. A sharp ache bolted through my skull, and I rubbed it as I tried to shush her. Of course, Stevie would not be shushed. "But I don't go hard, I go fast. I'm fast, Mommy, and he didn't even notice. He just said that if I couldn't even give one hard kick, I should quit sports."

"Did Mrs. B say why Mr. Dylan left?" I asked.

"He got fired," Dio said. "For saying the 'F' word."

I seethed. The word *freak* was never mentioned in Bewitcher's Beach. Too long had hunters used that cruel name to make those of us who were supernatural look bad. I wondered if it was the same creep who'd called the witch a freak.

Stevie nodded, her splayed hair tangling and knotting against the pillow. "He said I should be stronger because I'm one of those..." She whispered the *freak* word. Thankfully, Stevie didn't sound offended by this horrible occurrence.

But I was.

I was sick at the thought of a teacher saying such a thing to my precious daughter. Who would call a child a freak? Who would call anyone a freak except a bully? Or...a hunter.

My stomach revolted as my heart stuttered.

Though I squeezed my eyes shut, everything came into

view at once. A hunter—someone who would dare use the "F" word—would expect supernatural people to be stronger, just as Mr. Dylan said to Stevie.

And just as Chanel had said about herself...

One hard swing.

The variety of weapons Bart saw made sense for a hunter, and Chanel—poor Chanel. Fear had radiated off of her, but it wasn't about environmental damage; it was likely because of a threat.

"Chanel's boyfriend," I whispered. He was mysterious, hidden in the shadows, and maybe not a boyfriend at all. When I showed up at her shop that day, she smelled anxious, not like a woman in love. Despite the cloud of jasmine perfume, I'd smelled the truth.

"What'd you say, Mom?" Dio asked.

Stevie had slipped into sleep. Her breaths came peacefully, unbothered—for now. A hunter was in our midst, but why? And why kill Ryan? He wasn't a supernatural person.

A thought struck me harder and more painful than the top bunk against my head. What if he wasn't after Ryan? Hattie had said I looked like him. From behind, we had the same hair, the same height. He was alone in Mockbuster when the killer hit him.

And the video tape...*the warning*. Could it be related? A dozen thoughts flashed through my mind at once. The speeding car, the shadows in the alley behind my shop. But how did the vampire bat fit into all of this? Would an animal really bond with a hunter? I didn't believe it was possible.

"Nothing," I said as I crouched and popped a gentle kiss on Dio's forehead. "Sleep well."

Bolting down into the shop, I snatched the video tape from the register and shoved it into the VCR. At the same time, I grabbed the phone off the receiver with my free hand. I didn't even look at the keys when I mashed Sett's cell phone number into the phone.

The line trilled and trilled as my foot tapped and tapped.

One hard swing.

Stevie had said Mr. Dylan was only good at baseball. Bart mentioned a baseball bat. Could the murder weapon be sports equipment? Ryan's blood was on the VCR, but Chanel could have set up that part of the story. She'd set up the entire scene of vampire suggestions using makeup and a crucifix and bulbs of garlic, possibly while under the barrel of a hunter's gun.

When the screen blinked on and the VCR rolled the tape, a woman appeared in front of me. Her small black eyes stared into the camera. She wore a heavy cape draped over her shoulders, and when she spoke, fangs poked out from beneath her top lip. One of her fangs sat slightly crooked, pointing inward like a pigeoned-toed tooth.

"This is a warning—"

My viewing was cut off by the click of the back door falling shut.

I startled, snapping my attention to the door beneath the spiral staircase. The flap of erratic wings fluttered quietly, only loud enough for my wolf ears to pinpoint.

In the shadows, a figure emerged, and every horrifying theory I had was confirmed. A man in a baseball cap wielded a steel bat in one hand and a pistol in the other, just like Chanel.

When he stepped into the dim light filtering in from the front windows, I vaguely recognized his pale blue eyes and bulging biceps. Dylan had been one of my customers, but I didn't recognize him then.

My mouth popped open, but it was he who spoke first.

"You're hard to catch, Ms. Titan."

CHAPTER 19
UNFAMILIAR FAMILY

MY FIRST REACTION to being called Ms. Titan was to correct him. But what use was correcting my murderer? He'd come here to hunt me down, not get my real name. Of course... Noema Titan *was* my real name, and this cold-blooded killer knew it.

My mouth popped open, and the only thing that came out was a single word. "Why?"

Dylan's grin spread wide and dripped with cruelty. "Every Titan must die."

I sucked in a razor-sharp breath.

Everything fell to the pit of my stomach. Any sense of security had been ripped out from under me. Suddenly, I missed the crowds, the bustling streets, the tourists milling about both the sidewalks and the park late into the night.

If the chilly wind and threat of rain hadn't driven them away or inside, there'd be witnesses—I wouldn't be alone.

Dylan cocked the gun as he stopped in front of me. "I didn't believe it when Holden said there was one left. You're the last Titan, the last problem, the last person standing in our way. But it all ends tonight." Twitching the pistol, he gestured for me to come out from behind the desk.

But I didn't move, not yet. My mind was spinning as I pieced the puzzle together.

Holden. This was the name of the hunter who'd disguised himself as a professor at Shadowvale University. We'd caught him trying to kill the witches there in a sorry attempt to stop the recreation of the protection spell. And here stood his friend.

The sound of fluttering wings tickled in my ears again. When my wolf ears shifted toward the noise, the movement caught Dylan's gaze.

He flicked his attention back to my face, frowning in disgust. "Don't you dare think of shifting, you freak. I have silver bullets too, and I know what you pulled on Holden." He stretched his arm, reaching the gun out across the desk. "That's why I'm close; you can't outrun a bullet coming from a gun that's only inches away."

I bristled, but only halfway. My attention was split between him and the little creature flying in the air behind him. I watched it, mesmerized for a moment.

The bat bared its tiny, gleaming fangs. One was crooked. I blinked, narrowing in on the creature again. The earnest look in its beady black eyes looked just like the vampire woman in the video.

I tuned into the voice of the woman on the screen. The volume was low, but I heard every word.

"I can't show my face," she said. "They're hunting us, and this will draw attention to Bewitcher's Beach."

As if in response to the video, the bat covered its face with its wing, then promptly went back to flapping its wings to stay in flight.

Smoky anger suddenly flooded the room, and Dylan

smacked the baseball bat against the desktop. I jumped at the impact that left a dent next to Mockbuster's register.

"Get out from behind there!" He spat.

"Why not just shoot me?" I asked. Keeping a killer talking kept them from killing, and truthfully, I wanted to know if he only had one silver bullet.

He laughed darkly. "Don't tempt me. I know your tricks. You freaks bait us into being devoured. Even with a silencer, guns are loud for freaks with super hearing. It'll alert all your little wolf and vampire friends and whatever else."

The bat bared its fangs again. And then again.

She was trying to tell me something, but what? If Stevie were here, she'd understand. What did Stevie always say?

Just watch the little things.

I tried not to look at the bat for too long to keep Dylan from noticing her. Watching just long enough, I saw her tilt her head back as if in a howl. Then she snapped her tiny jaws at the air in Dylan's direction and waved her wing toward herself.

I'd gathered that the bat wanted me to transform while she went in for a bite. But Dylan's gun was right on me. Was I fast enough?

I didn't have time to overthink it. The bat screeched as it darted for Dylan's neck. With her jaws spread wide, she closed her mouth over his throat, sinking her fangs into the soft flesh just beneath his scratchy chin. I dropped to all fours, ducking behind the desk as if it were a shield. Stacks of video tapes clattered around me as I found my footing with my paws.

In reaction to the bite, he grunted in pain and his finger tightened over the trigger, firing the bullet from its chamber.

The gunshot exploded all around me in a boom that'd radiate through my wolf ears for hours.

The bullet buried in the TV screen that was right behind where my head had been. Glass shattered and sprinkled down on me in tiny shards. Like spiky, dangerous rain, the pieces fell harmlessly against my thick fur, but as they scattered across the carpet, I couldn't move without embedding the glass into my paws.

Dylan shouted a string of curses and fired the gun again. This time the bullet penetrated the glass on the front door. I yelped and wanted to duck under the cover of the desk, hiding myself between the towers of video tapes, but the bat needed my help taking him down.

The bat chirped, and I caught sight of it fluttering in the air before it dived at him again. He shouted near-unintelligible profanity, then released a scream of pain as something clattered to the floor.

I peered around the desk to see the baseball bat lying harm-lessly on the floor. Dylan scrabbled at the vampire bat on his neck with one hand while he twisted the gun, turning it on the creature. If he fired, he'd kill her.

I lunged from behind the desk, catching my hip against the edge of it. But I didn't slow. Instead, I launched into the air, my paws aiming for the center of his chest and my jaws open wide. I was ready to snap down on his hand, leaving his fingers limp and unable to use the gun at all. If he couldn't flex his fingers, he couldn't pull the trigger.

Closing my canines over his hand, he screamed again, and the cry of agony seared through my ears. The gun fell from his hold, and he slammed against the carpet, my paws planted on top of his collarbone.

The bat released him, fluttering into the air again. Her form transformed before my eyes, wings vanishing, tiny fangs extending, claws becoming feet and hands as a fully-human—vampire—body manifested before me.

An enchanted cloak modestly covered her, molding around

her movement as she became a blur. She dropped to a crouch, snatching the gun from between her feet.

Training it on Dylan now, she glanced at me for a moment. I could have sworn she flashed me a smile before her red lips bent into a frown.

"You're wrong," she said. "Noema is not the last Titan woman."

I THOUGHT my heart would burst as I stared at the woman in front of me. I didn't know her, nor did I recognize her face beyond the quick second I saw of her on the screen, but something within me warmed.

Something within me knew her.

I was speechless. Even when I ducked behind the cover of the front desk to shift back into my human form and slip into my clothes, I didn't make a sound.

When Sett arrived, I didn't speak to him. When he arrested Dylan, locking handcuffs around his wrists, and Dylan snapped at me, I didn't bite back.

When the vampire woman turned to me, forming my name on her tongue, I didn't respond. I only stared at her.

"I'm sorry it had to be this way," she said. Her black eyes welled with brief tears that she quickly blinked away. "But it's so good to see you. To talk to you like this, even if we shouldn't."

"We shouldn't?" I whispered, finding my words again.

As Sett shoved Dylan to his feet, Doctor Pitt ducked into the shop, carrying his medical bag. Having heard the gunshots, Hattie and Bette surged into Mockbuster through Everland Theater's shared wall.

Onlookers from The Oyster Inn gathered outside to peer through the glass and see what all the commotion was about. Dylan had been right; the noise of the gun firing drew a small crowd. But the vampire had been there all along, slipping in behind him when he broke through the back door to hunt me down.

She'd been following me, attacking me even, all this time, like a little leathery guardian angel with a fierce bite.

"I'm afraid I should go," she said. "Before more hunters find out I'm still alive." Glancing at the front and the flood of people now invading our space, she took a step toward the back door.

I reached out and touched her arm gingerly, afraid she'd transform back into a bat and fly out of my reach. "Wait."

Her dark eyes glittered, catching the flashing blue and red lights of the cop car parked on the curb out front. Her gaze trailed to the chaos around us, and I followed her line of sight. Sett pushed Dylan in that direction, yanking open the door and placing a hand on the killer's head so that he wouldn't hit the car as he dropped into the back seat.

"It isn't safe here," she said. "Not until the entire hoard is found."

"The hoard?"

"The video will tell you all," she said. "I'm sorry I had to bite you, and for every time I came after you. You weren't understanding my message, and getting you away from danger was more important. Each time I showed up, he was close by, and I wanted you to flee to safety, but I couldn't risk you by revealing myself. I'm also sorry that I can't spend time with you." Water pooled at her bottom eyelids again. "I wish more than anything in the world that I could stay and get to know who you are now, Noema. I've been watching out for you since I heard you were still alive. I adore Jovi, and Dio, and Halen, and Stevie..." Her voice choked. She quickly glanced up at the top of the staircase, where four curious faces peered out of the crack between the loft's door frame and the door. "Stevie looks just like her grandmother."

My pulse skipped. "She does?"

She smiled softly, wrinkles crinkling at the corners of her eyes. "Without the wolf ears, yes. And you, Noema, are exactly the kind of woman I knew you'd grow up to be."

Tears blurred my vision. "Are we..." Emotion caught in my throat. Could she be part of my family? "Are we related?"

"Since becoming a vampire, my aging has slowed, so this might be hard to believe, but...I'm your grandmother."

Sett returned to the shop, striding over to us with purpose and a notepad and a look of fierce concern on his face.

"And now," she said. "I have to go."

"No!" I reached out for her again, but she shifted into a bat and swooped past Sett and out the open door. Onlookers ducked as the bat fluttered over their heads and disappeared into the night sky.

My grandmother.

"Are you okay?" Sett asked. It seemed he'd said those same words to me a hundred times.

I'd always nodded before. Even when I was bitten, I didn't admit total defeat, but now...

"No," I whispered. Tears burned in my eyes again. The bridge of my nose tingled with intense emotion. My children had spotted another member of their family for the first time tonight, and they couldn't even meet her. I spoke with my real-life—well, undead—grandmother. And just like that, she's already gone.

Without another word, Sett lifted his heavy arms. Encircling me with his strength, he pulled me close, letting me bury my face into his broad chest. It didn't matter that I went limp in his arms; he kept me standing, upright, supported. Always.

Right there, in front of tourists and children, friends and the family I'd made in Bewitcher's Beach, I let the tears fall. Sobs didn't rack me, but my crying was steady, silent, and full of confusion. The bright scent of joy lifted my spirits, but with it came a multitude of other smells. Pineapple pizza, rain, and key lime pie swirled in the air around us.

I was as confused about this brief meeting as I was sad that I had to watch her go. But the hope remained, a constant light in the dark of this wild night.

Hope to see her again. Hope to meet the rest of my family. Hope that even if I didn't marry a reaper or live up to the prophecies mentioning my fate, I was still Noema Titan.

Tears fell until I was too dehydrated and tired to cry any longer. Sett released me, and I wiped at my nose, looking up at him with a hint of guilt shifting the air around me. Too long had he lingered here when there was business to attend to.

"You have to go deal with Dylan now, right?" I asked.

"It can wait," he said. "I protect first, process second."

"I'm safe now," I said. I dropped my head, wiping at my face with my palms.

He used the edge of his finger to tip my chin up to face him again. "Protection is about support too. And, Noema, I've never seen you with so few words." The ghost of a smile crossed his face.

I almost smiled. "So you're saying it's obvious that I'm not fine?"

"Very obvious. The Noema I know talks so much that she doesn't know what speechless even means."

A strange bubbling laugh came out of me in one huff. All the emotion welled up inside of me, and the tension tightening my muscles released at once. My shoulders deflated.

"Why didn't you go after the vampire? For a statement, I mean. She was holding the gun when you got here."

"Because of you. Your body language and behavior suggested she was helping you. I suspect she was the bat who has been following you."

I nodded. "She's my—" I swallowed. "Kind of like my guardian angel, but she said she was my grandmother." Confusion creased his brow. "I know that's a good thing. I'm excited but also sad and I don't know what to think. She was helping me, and then she just ran away. Or, I guess she flew away. You know what I mean."

"This is the Noema I know." I shot him a look, and he merely smirked.

"I could go on about it, but I'm exhausted. I'm assuming I need to make an official statement and all that jazz?"

"That would be helpful, but there's no rush."

I bit my lip as the dang tears came flooding back. I thought I'd cried myself dry only to stand here filling up like a cup at the faucet again. "It's just—she left me, *again*."

Sett swallowed me again, pulling me into the cool relief of his hug. His body was rough and solid, but his touch was always soft. He was like a firm pillow, a place to land when I needed rest.

"I said there's no rush, Noema. Let yourself grieve for a second."

There's no rush. How had I never appreciated Sett's pace before? I'd been irritated with him so many times. Never grateful enough for his calming presence.

"She's not dead. I'm not grieving."

"Noema, I've lost family before. They don't have to be buried for you to grieve."

I pulled back, my lips parting as I stared up at him. "You have?"

"It's a story for another time." He dropped his arms, slipping his hands into his coat pockets instead of around me. "For now, I have good news. Rufus didn't exactly turn himself in the way his wife claimed he would, but he's here and he confessed to assaulting you. He ran because he thought you were trying to hurt him when you became a werewolf. So he grabbed his wife and they dodged out of town to get away from you, only to hear that the cops were looking for him. He came back to straighten the story out."

"And?" I asked. "Is it straight?"

"He doesn't want to see you again, let's just say that, so he offered you a deal and asked if I could present it to you."

I shuffled uncomfortably, my gaze darting to Hattie, who still hovered behind Sett to make sure I was okay. She gave me a curt nod. Whatever choice Rufus offered, apparently it was my decision.

"If you don't press charges," he continued, "any money that he'd have to pay for the charges will be donated to Everland Theater along with what he's already given. He just doesn't want his name tied to it, for now. He said you'd know what that means. It feels slimy, if you ask me."

"Tell him it's a deal," I said.

Maybe Rufus was a little slimy, but I wasn't going to drop the plan for Everland Theater's big screen. Rufus's projects were failing because supernaturals lived in communities like Bewitcher's Beach all over the world. Towns this small didn't feature movie theaters, so supernatural films failed at the box office.

I was going to change that, whether I liked change or not.

CHAPTER 20
THEY'RE COMING

WIND TOSSED brittle leaves across the cobblestone. The crowds had left Bewitcher's Beach in their wake, and I finally had a second to write that last scene. The dust settled in my screenplay at the same time that it did in town. For now.

With only two weeks until the fall festival, I had no doubt tourists would return in droves for pumpkin flavored taffy and the debut of Everland Theater. We announced that we'd premiere a new movie called *Halloweentown*, which was set to release on TV this October but not in any theaters—except ours —and I couldn't wait.

I locked the door to Mockbuster and hurried upstairs, where Sett and the kids waited. While Stevie, Dio, Halen, and Jovi piled around the small kitchen table stacked with pumpkins, safety knives and buckets in hand, Sett dropped into the old couch in our family room. The cushions bent under Sett's weight, and the wood creaked when he scooted aside to make room for me.

"They're going to make a huge mess," I said, nodding toward the kitchen.

"I covered everything in newspapers, and they each have a gut bucket."

I frowned. "Gross."

With a laugh, he explained that the pumpkin carving contest he'd challenged them to would be the perfect distraction. He tilted his head. "I know this can be heavy for them. If you don't think the pumpkin project is enough to keep them busy, we can wait until tomorrow when they're back in school."

I sank into the couch beside him and stared at the TV. The video tape was already inserted into my brand new VCR. Shaking my head, I reached for the remote. "No, I've waited long enough."

The push and pull of emotions, the hype and then rapid loss of my grandmother's presence in my life, left me raw. I felt like a flayed open fish and probably smelled like one too with how much I guilt I'd suffered over the delay. This video could have important information that would lead to catching other criminals like Dylan and Professor Holden. We knew hunters were out there, but their hiding skills had improved.

Sett, ever patient, allowed me to wait until I was ready to see my grandmother's face again. This time, she'd be distanced with the screen between us, not a flesh and blood being that I could reach out and touch.

It took a couple weeks, but I'd gathered the courage to face the flood of emotions that I'd dammed up with distractions. Hattie was right; in order to have more—to know more—I had to accept a little change.

And I had no doubt that whatever I was about to learn about my family and myself from this video would change my life.

"Are you sure you're ready?" Sett asked.

I shrugged. "No, but nobody is ever ready for change." I lifted the remote and hit play.

The TV blinked, and my grandmother appeared on the screen. She sat in a dim room, a bookshelf full of cracked, leather-bound tomes behind her. Her velvety dress draped over her crossed legs, and her fingernails were painted green. With a grim smile, she revealed the tips of her fangs. This woman was the picture perfect combination of witch and vampire.

"This is a warning. Please listen carefully for no other reason than that I love you."

Emotion lumped in my throat like a fist painfully squeezing everything out of me. My eyes threatened to leak. I didn't even know this woman, but she seemed to know me and love me.

Sett's cool hand reached into my lap and found mine. Lacing his fingers through mine, he gave my hand a gentle squeeze. I didn't dare look at him. If I saw so much as a hint of care in his eyes, I wouldn't be able to keep the floodgates closed. This was already too much.

My grandmother continued. "Once we found out that you were alive, I took care to make sure you'd never find out that you were a Titan woman. This was for your own protection. I couldn't bear to rip you away from your life, but I didn't want to risk your life either. It had to stay a secret. The less you know, the better. I can't show my face anywhere near here. They're hunting us, and this will draw attention to Bewitcher's Beach.

"What I can tell you now is that there's a hoard of over a hundred hunters who've branded the Titan family their mortal enemies. The news surrounding the arrest of a professor at Shadowvale University alerted me that you were close to finding the truth." She clasped her hands in front of her, resting them on her crossed knee. Staring into the camera, she locked onto my soul. "Noema, if I know where you are, so do they. Hunters will be coming. One by one, they'll try, so they don't draw the attention of law enforcement. They'll keep it quiet, sneaky, framing others when they can."

I thought of Chanel. Poor Chanel. She was released now and took a holiday with her boys at her sisters' house in Monterey. There, she'd enjoy some of the cleanest and most beautiful beaches with the other sirens. I only hoped she'd feel safe and comfortable enough to return and resume business at her boutique in Bewitcher's Beach. It wouldn't feel right with her shop shut down for too long.

Maybe Madam Rowena and the witches of Shadowvale would be here soon to cast the new protection spell. Maybe Bewitcher's Beach would be safe again, and before the fall festival. Madam Rowena had said they were only days away from completing the spell, and I was only moments away from calling her with every word my grandmother said.

"The hunters are out for revenge, but they want so much more than that. They believe you're the last Titan woman alive, the key, the last witch who can seal the protection spell that will take away their ability to hunt forever."

My grandmother leaned closer to the camera and my heart skipped. "Noema, they'll stop at nothing to kill you, and soon, the whole hoard will be flooding Bewitcher's Beach. Rest assured, I'll be working to find a way to stop them. I'll do everything I can for you and for our family."

My entire insides were knotted up, and I didn't realize I was squeezing the life out of Sett's hand until he squeezed back.

I glanced at our intertwined fingers and then at his face. "Sorry."

"Don't be." He squeezed my hand again. "Give me all you've got."

I hoped he meant it, because when my grandmother spoke again, she broke my heart. "I wish I could tell you more about us, but it's safer this way. You must know, though, that your mother loves you deeply. So very deeply. And so do I. Everything about you, your impatience, your fervor, your wild spirit, and your fierce mama's heart says that you're a Titan woman. But please, be careful with that name. There is a prophecy for you to marry, and marry quickly; this change in your name will help conceal you as it did for me. When I married, everybody knew me as Lulu Ambrosia."

Lulu! I squeezed Sett's hand so hard, my fingers ached. If this was the Lulu who wrote *The Book of Prophecies* and created the protection spell, why couldn't she help the witches at Shadowvale? The sooner we had a magical layer of protection, the sooner she could stop running away and hiding.

But like she said, there was still so much I didn't know. About her. About magic. About myself.

I was the key, whatever that meant.

"You should do the same," Lulu continued. "Marry quickly and wrap your family into his. This is your fate. In prophecies, mentioning death is a way of hinting at urgency. This means that our time is nearly up. The word 'reaper' is a clue, but the prophecy's plain English does not mean what you think it means. Marry quickly, Noema, but marry for love."

My entire body suddenly burned, and I yanked my hand away from Sett. Chanel's words needled me again.

He loves you.

I dared to steal a glance at him only to find he was staring right back.

Stevie's sharp cry startled us from our shared gaze. She stomped into the family room with a fistful of pumpkin guts.

"It's ruined! I tried cutting the shape of a frog, and the eyes looked like squares!" She climbed onto the couch between us, burying her face in Sett's thick arm as she let the tears fall. She was a mirror of me only a couple of weeks before, when I cried in Sett's arms.

He released my hand and wrapped an arm around her

shoulders, crushing her in a quick hug. When he let go, he pushed to his feet and held out his hand as an offer for her to take it and follow him back into the kitchen. "That's why I got an extra pumpkin for each of you."

Stevie launched off the couch and barreled past him into the kitchen. "Will you help me cut it out?" She shouted as she ran.

"Of course." He laughed as he strode toward the kitchen, but not without a glance back at me. Mouthing the words, he said his favorite phrase. *Are you okay?*

I didn't have an answer. I wasn't entirely okay. A hoard of hunters was coming for me, and I had no doubt Sett would dive into that investigation the moment the pumpkin carving was complete. But for tonight, we couldn't do anything about my missing family or the hunters they were running from.

For tonight, I'd enjoy a simple evening with loved ones before the changing of the tides.

THANK YOU FOR READING!
JOIN NOEMA FOR ANOTHER ENCHANTING MYSTERY
IN *WITCHES, WALKIE TALKIES, AND WARNINGS: BOOK 6 OF
THE BEWITCHER'S BEACH PARANORMAL COZY MYSTERIES!*

PLEASE CONSIDER LEAVING A REVIEW AT YOUR FAVORITE PLACE TO PURCHASE BOOKS!

ALSO, A SHARE WITH YOUR FRIENDS WHO LOVE TO LAUGH AND SOLVE MYSTERIES WOULD BE

GREATLY APPRECIATED. MY QUEST AS AN AUTHOR IS TO MAKE OTHERS FEEL SEEN THROUGH THE ADVENTURE OF FICTION. PLEASE REACH OUT TO ME AND LET ME KNOW IF MY STORIES HAVE TOUCHED YOU. YOU, DEAR READER, ARE WHO THIS BOOK WAS WRITTEN FOR.

BEWITCHER'S BEACH
RECIPES

SETT'S 'WEREWOLF SAFE' GRANOLA BARS

When to eat: when life is so busy that you actually agree to let the impatient werewolf mom help catch a murderer.

Ingredients:

- 2 ½ cups oats
- ¼ cup chopped almonds
- ⅓ cup maple syrup
- ¼ cup butter
- ½ cup brown sugar
- ½ tsp vanilla extract
- ¼ tsp salt
- ½ cup peanut butter chips
- (optional) ⅓ cup of dried fruit ·

Instructions:

- Preheat the oven to 350 degrees.
- Chop almonds and fruit (if using).
- Bake oats and almonds for 4-5 minutes. Toss bake another 4-5 minutes. Move to bowl.
- Heat butter, brown sugar, vanilla, and salt on stove.
- Stir and pour over oats and almond mixture. Mix.
- After allowing to cool, add peanut butter chips and fruits.
- Flatten granola on a baking pan lined with parchment paper.
- Freeze for 30 minutes.
- Cut granola into bars. Store in fridge for up to 7 days.
- Enjoy on the go!

ABOUT THE AUTHOR

Congenital Heart Defect survivor, Emily Fluke, finds joy and peace through the expression of writing. She is a firm believer that all stories need a little magic and a lot of excitement. Emily and her husband spend their free time wrangling two children and playing video games in their busy California lifestyle. Otherwise, you'll find Emily solving an escape room, running, or writing Magic the Gathering-based poetry.

To stay up to date on new releases and connect with me, visit my website at Emilyfluke.com or follow me on social media under Author Emily Fluke, or @emilyflukefairytales.